Other Titles by Joe Cacciotti

Hurricane Strips Las Vegas

Hurricane Rocks Wisconsin

Poems for the Heart II

Poems for the Heart

Blue Collar Real Estate Mogul

Coming Soon

Hurricane Volunteers in Tennessee

Hurricane Strikes Rhode Island

Hurricane Mashes Idaho

Hurricane Gold Rushes California

Poems for the Heart III

HURRICANE
Cores the Big Apple

joseph j. cacciotti

1

SECOND EDITION

Marbry Books

Hurricane Cores the Big Apple
SECOND EDITION

By Joseph J. Cacciotti

All characters and events in this book are completely fictional and a product of the author's own imagination.

Paperback: ISBN: 978-1-938526-55-8
eBook: ISBN: 978-1-938526-56-5
ePub: ISBN: 978-1-938526-57-2
Mobi: ISBN: 978-1-938526-58-9

Published by:

Marbry Books
P.O. Box 894
Locust Grove, Georgia 30248 USA
www.MarbryBooks.com

This book may be purchased from TheLaurusCompany.com, Amazon.com, and other retailers around the world.

In memory of my friend
Harold A. Schink

Chapter One

The mounting tension leading up to Y2K six months prior had dissipated like a fine mist in the rising sun. The end had not come, the world's collective sigh was noted, and by now the turning of a new century was forgotten by New Yorkers as yesterday's news. June had arrived and with it the Atlantic hurricane season.

Detective Sam Rufus folded like a jackknife at the sound of his alarm clock and placed his feet on the soft carpeting of his 31st floor Manhattan apartment. On his way to the front door to retrieve the stack of dailies, he stepped into the kitchen and switched on the Krups. Then he crossed the living room to throw open the balcony doors. The sun's first rays stretched across his muscled frame, and he breathed in the coolest air of the day. It was a troubled breath, however, the kind that comes with waking and remembering. It became more ragged as the bold headline stared up at him from the *Staten Island Advance*, "Seventh Staten Islander Slain in Seven Days."

The paper's front page mirrored the half dozen others he skimmed each morning while downing two cups of black coffee. He flipped open the paper and saw a photo of himself and a fellow detective after cracking an airport parking lot sniper case that had rolled on for several months. It seemed like no matter what rag you picked up lately, there he was, and depending upon which story you read, Sam Rufus, aka Hurricane, was either a hero, a renegade, or a raving lunatic.

In five short years with the NYPD, three of them on the streets, Sam had gained a reputation for unorthodox, truth-and-justice-seeking methods. No matter how he looked in print or what people said about him, they all agreed that he always got the job done. And right now, it seemed that Staten Island had a mighty big job they needed him to do.

Seven citizens had been slain in seven days, each one with a clean shot to the heart. Even two kids had been killed, along with their father, as they stepped out their front door. It was unbelievable. Someone was picking people off methodically in daylight in a relatively concentrated area without leaving a clue. It grieved Sam that the killer, or killers, remained at large. The air on the Island was so thick with panic that people were afraid to leave their homes, and for good reason. So, why had they not called him in on the case? All of the law enforcement agencies in and around New York City practiced interagency cooperation, and the bureau chief knew that Sam Rufus could root out vermin invisible to others and was a solver of complex crimes, just like his father had been.

Five years earlier, Sam had opted out of another four-year stint with the Green Berets and returned to Manhattan upon learning that his father was seriously ill. He wanted to be close to home in case his parents needed him. Sam had been extremely proud of his father. Everywhere they went, from west to east and as early as Sam could remember, people had been drawn to his father and would stop to talk. His father involved himself with others, especially strangers and people who were different from him. He didn't care who or what they were; they all mattered and deserved respect. They all had a story worth hearing, and they all were a part of the same great family, as far as he was concerned.

Arthur Rufus had been a big man, standing six-four, with massive arms and a vice-grip strength he had developed during his years in the military. After twenty years of service, he retired from the U.S. Army, came home to Manhattan with his wife and children, and joined the police force. He quickly climbed the ladder, was promoted to lieutenant, and then moved into the Detective Bureau. As a boy, Sam wanted to be just like his father when he grew up, or some combination of him, Mike Hammer, and MacGyver all wrapped up into one.

Sam questioned with humor the fairness of his sister getting their father's height, while he had drawn the short straw. He figured he took more after his mother who she was short, maybe five-foot at best. She had always told him that good things came in small packages. He couldn't argue that point because she could have passed for an angel. Sarah, his younger sister by almost two years, had married Charlie Watts, a lifetime friend Sam had made while they were in the Green Berets. Sarah and Charlie had fallen in love at first sight.

Sam remembered when Charlie first opened up to him. His parents had died instantly when a long-haul truck driver carrying a load of citrus fell asleep and crossed the center line, crashing head-on into their vehicle. Charlie was at school when it happened, twelve years old, and an only child. After the double funeral, he had been bounced between uncles and aunts in two-year intervals until he finished high school, fully convinced that the U.S. Army was equally as viable as going to college, and without the tuition expense.

In one of his weekly letters, Sam had told his mother about Charlie, and after that, she insisted that Sam bring him home when they had leave again. She would cook her specialty, Italian spaghetti, and feed them a real home-cooked meal.

When they walked into the house, Arthur shook Charlie's hand and welcomed him like a second son. After all, he was a Green Beret and a friend of Sam's. Sam's mother stepped out from Arthur's shadow and, after hugging Sam long and hard, reached for Charlie as well, saying, "Charlie, we're so happy you came. I hope you like spaghetti."

Moments later, Sam laughed out loud when his sister, whom he considered to be a real looker, joined them and Charlie's words stumbled and tripped over each other until he finally stopped mid-sentence and just stared at her. Charlie was as tough as tempered steel, but he had tottered and swayed and allowed himself to be blown over like a feather in the wind by Sam's kid sister.

All through supper, Charlie's eyes drifted across the table to Sarah's plate, up her blouse to her fine hazel eyes that twinkled back at him. He couldn't keep his eyes off of her. Sam's mother broke the spell when she said, "Charlie, Sam told us about the unfortunate loss of your parents."

"Thank you, Mrs. Rufus, but that was a long time ago," Charlie said.

"Please, call me Anna, or Mama, like Sam." She looked at him kindly and smiled.

9

"Thank you, Mrs. Rufus, uh, Anna, Mama." He looked at Sarah and blushed. "Now I know why Sam gets happy at the thought of coming home. This is the best food I've tasted in a long time. Thank you for inviting me."

The family joke about Sam's mother being Shoshone and cooking Italian was making the rounds when Anna said, "Then it's settled, Charlie. Every time you are on leave, you are welcome here, and I won't take no for an answer. Any friend of Sam's is a welcome guest in this house."

"How do you like the Green Berets, Charlie?" Arthur asked.

"I love it. There's nothing like it. It's the best thing that has ever happened to me, sir. I'm thinking of making it a career," Charlie answered.

A wide smile had spread across Arthur's face. "I was also a career man, Charlie. I was in the army for twenty years. I now have three years in the Manhattan Police Department and another five in the Bureau. By the time I retire, I'll have a twenty-twenty career. That's twenty years in the service and twenty years in NYPD. Not a bad retirement package."

Charlie looked thoughtful after Arthur's words, as if he might be seriously contemplating a similar future for himself, but when he looked at Arthur and opened his mouth to speak, he surprised himself and everyone else by what came out.

"Arthur, I'd like to ask your permission to date Sarah, sir."

Someone dropped a fork, and then there was complete silence while Charlie anxiously awaited an answer to his plea.

"What!" Arthur barked. "You just met her this evening. What could your intentions possibly be with my only daughter, Charlie? And before you answer that, let me warn you that this girl knows her martial arts. I taught her myself, and she can kick your butt from here to Chicago if she needs to keep you in line. Now, tell me, what is up with your intentions, and they better be good!"

"Wuh, why, I have the best intentions toward her, sir. She's the loveliest woman I've ever seen. I will treat her like a queen."

"Sure, sure, of course, you will. That is all well and good, but don't you think Sarah has a voice in all this, or are you taking those sparks that have been flying back and forth between the two of you all night to mean she is about as interested in you as you are in her?"

They all laughed, and the courtship started right then and there. Six months later when Charlie returned with Sam, he and Sarah tied the knot.

Arthur knew all about love at first sight. He had met Anna while he was at home on leave from the army and as sick as a dog with a fever that hovered at 104 degrees, refusing to break. He had lain hot as a rock on cool sheets in a room where the lights were too bright and hurt his eyes. Forms and voices had run together like watercolors on a canvas. When he was able to focus for the first time in nearly two weeks, she was standing quietly beside his bed, sponging his head and neck with cool water. She smiled comfort at him with her topaz eyes and spoke a soft sing-song of unfamiliar words to him. He was too weak to return the smile but watched her cat-like movements through heavy lids and memorized her touch. *She must be Indian*, he thought, and slept again.

The next day he was more awake, feeling stronger and more curious.

"Who are you, and what tribe are you?" he asked her.

"I am Anna Morning Star. I am Shoshone," she had told him.

As she delicately spooned nourishing broth into his mouth, he learned her family was in central Nevada, still on the reservation, and involved in the fight against all things nuclear, especially the current drama happening at the Nevada Test Site.

"I had to either get involved with the protest or get away from it and get a bigger look at things."

As Arthur's health rallied, she shared more of her history with him, describing the small reservation and how its population was consistently dwindling. She had left the reservation to go to nursing school on a government grant. It was part of an effort to educate her people so they would integrate better outside the reservation. In the sixties, when the country's military recruitment efforts for women were heavily underway, she had answered the call and joined the army, serving as a medical specialist."

Dang it, she's beautiful, he thought. Her skin was like smooth, polished cherry wood, her features fine and sculpted. He opened his mouth to the incoming spoon but intercepted her hand with his.

"I can do this now," he assured her.

She had been in the army for three and a half years and would return to the Shoshone reservation in another six months to put her nursing skills to use. "

Arthur was smitten. Don't ask me to explain it," he had warned the man in the next bed. He would need to get well and act fast.

With all the persuasive words in him he spoke his heart and overcame her quiet, sensible objections a day at a time until his strength returned and he was released from her care. When her four-year term ended, they married in the Nevada town of Ely and learned soon thereafter that Sam was on the way.

Sam spent his first six years with the Shoshone, and sister Sarah her first four. The Nevada desert was a perfect place for hands-on learning and home schooling. Indian boys were taught how to hunt, fish, and track practically before they could crawl, and Screaming Eagle, Sam's Shoshone name, was a quick study. Even though he was very young, he easily grasped the ways of the land and its inhabitants. He understood the sky with its cloud formations and fierce, sudden storms. He had learned the names of the wild plants and their uses. He could identify poisonous snakes by their markings and birds by the sound of their calls. Anna Morning Star made certain that her children spent time with people of all ages and that they showed proper respect for the Elders.

After his last two successive tours of duty, Arthur knew it was time to leave the army and move his family off the reservation and into mainstream America. With Anna's agreement, he accepted the assistance of his own family who, over a period of several months, prepared a place for them in Manhattan. Sam and Sarah would need a real education, and they would settle into a solid family life. He hoped that his frequent letters and less-frequent visits had prepared Anna for the drastic changes that were at hand. She opened her arms wide to the idea and excitedly prepared their children for their very different life.

Now, on this morning so many years later, Sam stood not far from where he had spent much of his boyhood. He had followed closely in his father's footsteps, and even though his military years added up to less, his skills had been honed laser sharp. He had made detective, then moved on to the homicide squad in record time, and now was proving himself one hundred percent invincible to every department.

He looked again at the headlines of the newspapers spread out around him. They were discouraging, maddening. All this death and disaster, for what purpose? A war was being waged across the small bay, a different kind of battle, a guerilla war where civilians were killing civilians. There was no honor or civility in that sort of war. A killer was out there somewhere in Staten Island, a despicable character with no conscience who was inflicting unjustifiable horror. People had a right to scream that their streets weren't safe, and they had a right to demand on the front pages of their newspapers, "Where Are Our Police?"

"That's right," Sam thought irritably. "Where are they?" He knew, however, that there were plenty of other detectives already involved in the case, just as they should be. But the killer was still on the loose. There were no witnesses, there were no suspects, and no one had unearthed enough evidence to sniff at or leads to exhaust. It drove him crazy. He knew there had to be traces of evidence somewhere. He wanted in on this case, and he would push that point with the chief when he confronted him in the station this morning.

Chapter Two

At the Staten Island Sheriff Department's Major Crimes Unit, Sheriff Jim Griggs and Deputy Clint Jones poured over printouts and crime scene reports just coming in. It was four o'clock in the morning. They were as baffled and outraged as the rest of the public and even more so now. Though the streets were being tightly watched and everyone was on high alert, another life had been claimed less than two hours ago.

The mayor was on the phone. He had been called at home and alerted to the news, and he was as mad as a swarm of African bees. He wanted answers, and he wanted them *now*. He would get them from the guy in whose back yard it was going down. Griggs would not mince words. He would respond well to a good grilling about what was being done to stop the killing.

"Despite all of the technology and our combined efforts with other agencies, including the FBI," Griggs told him, "there's little evidence available. Victims were all DOA. Crime scenes were clean as a whistle, and nothing was left in their wake except a lot of blood and a few bullet casings from a 30/30 Winchester rifle. We were unable to get any prints off of them. Look, Mayor, you've got to know that we're doing the best we can with what we have. Nobody is sitting around idly twiddling their thumbs. We have …" Griggs drew a long breath and then talked without pausing for a solid five minutes, updating the mayor with the investigative actions.

"I'm about ready to call on a man who might be able to help us. He's already on the force as a top detective, but for some reason, he's been kept busy and away from this. Go figure. You know him. Just about everyone knows him. He's no shrinking violet in his style of police work, and he always gets the job done."

"I don't care what you have to do or who you have to lean on to get it done. Just get it done!" With that, the mayor was gone, and Jim Griggs sat quietly questioning his own judgment.

Deputy Jones broke the silence. "What's going on up there in your head, Jim?"

"I'm thinking it's time to call in my friend, Sam Rufus. I just got the green light from the mayor."

"Wait just a minute. Who did you say you're going to call?" It was a voice from just outside his door. "Are you trying to tell me this one man you're thinking of calling can find who you, your men, NYPD detectives, and my agents can't?" FBI Agent Johnson had poked his head in the sheriff's open door and now stood before him to finish the point.

"I'm not trying to put your agency, your men, or anybody else down, Johnson, but this is no ordinary situation, and this is no ordinary man. He's highly-trained ex-military, rose to the top of the detective bureau in warp speed, and you won't find a better tracker or marksman anywhere in the world." There was a slight tone of annoyance in the sheriff's voice.

"Who are you talking about? If he's that good, why haven't we heard of him, and why isn't he working with us?" Agent Johnson asked.

"Oh, you've heard of him. Unless you've avoided the news altogether for the past year, you couldn't have missed him. Like I said, he's cream that rose to the top quickly. Aced the tests, paid his dues in patrol and probation, and practically raised the dead in investigations. He's on the top, and all in about five years. Now he's carving a niche of his own, an odd niche but an unmistakable one. His old man was NYPD, too, but nothing's taken the department by storm quite like him. He breathes rare air. You've heard of him, all right."

"Hey, Jim," Clint said, "Are you talking about that guy from Manhattan who's been in the newspapers more times than Britney Spears?"

Before Griggs could answer, Clint went on, "I read about him. They call him the Twister or the Hurricane or something like that."

"That's right, Clint. You're talking about Hurricane Sam Rufus," Sheriff Griggs stated. A smile flickered ever so slightly over his face.

"You know him personally then, do you?"

"Know him! Hell, I grew up with him. Some people are saying he's the meanest, lowest person out there and that he's got an axe to grind. He's getting himself a reputation as a lone wolf, and he's accumulated a pretty unusual arsenal. When he draws his gun or anything else, he draws it to use it," Jim said, daring Clint to think about what they were getting into.

"That's exactly why we need him," Clint said. "You name me any person in New York who would have the guts to hunt down a killer alone on these lonely streets."

"It sounds a little simple, but you may have a point. I don't like to be out on the streets like this with an entire team, much less being out there alone. Maybe if the killer sees less of us, some nut-case lone stealth that's not afraid of his shadow will have better luck," Agent Johnson said.

Clint turned his attention back to Sheriff Griggs. "Were the two of you good friends?"

"We were the best of friends from sixth grade on, and then he enlisted in the army, which is another story. Time and distance naturally took their toll, and now, besides talking a few times a year by phone to play catch-up, we haven't seen each other since his father passed nearly five years ago. Where does the time go?"

Jim told them his memories of when Sam and his family had moved in next door to him. It had been Sam's second move in Manhattan, and his room this time was almost the entire finished basement of their house. They were the same age, but Sam was different from anyone he knew or had ever met. Sam knew things his other friends didn't, and he was fearless, more fearless than most twelve-year-old boys. Maybe it was because he'd spent his earliest years living with his mother on an Indian reservation out West. Or maybe it was because his dad was a giant with tree trunks for arms and was a cop to boot. At first, Jim hadn't seen too much of either of them. Sam's dad was on the police force and wasn't home that much, but when he was, he spent a lot of time with Sam. He would take him to the gym for a few hours, and when they returned, Sam would go into the back yard and start spinning and kicking and punching the air.

"I used to watch him from my bedroom window and try to mimic his moves. He could spin like a top, firing jabs so fast from his hands and feet that you could hardly see them. Both he and his sister were being taught

17

martial arts by their father and one of his good friends who owned a small gym in the Village. He wanted Sam to know how to protect his mother when he wasn't home, and he wanted Sarah to be able to take care of herself."

"Sam had a goofy side, too," Jim remembered. "There was Sam the entertainer, carrying a tambourine with him almost everywhere he went. On our way home from school, Sam would pause on street corners and sing goofy songs he made up on the spot. He would shuffle his feet and twist around—he called it dancing—and hold out a cap for tips. He wasn't half bad, and a few people threw him money, but only the kind that jingles. There was Sam the artist. Sam and his Sharpie pens embellished any poster anywhere he could get away with it. He was a master painter of moles and mustaches. There was Sam the real estate magnate. He had a thing for taking For Sale signs from one yard and putting them in another. One time, he had a half dozen signs from different agencies in one yard. There were so many things, and of course, no friend would leave another out there hanging in the breeze all by himself." Jim admitted coming along for the ride and the inspiration.

"Sam was smart," he said looking at Clint. "He knew things. And school was way too easy for him. He had to become the entertainer, artist, and entrepreneur to keep from falling asleep. That's how he struck me."

Jim's mind was moving toward the one time they weren't so lucky, but Clint's voice snapped him out of his reverie. "Huh?"

"I said, 'How did he ever get the name Hurricane?'" Clint repeated.

"I was getting to that. I already told you I was twelve when Sam's family moved in next door to us. They had been there only a few days, and I wasn't even sure he was my neighbor until one Friday morning on the way back home from my paper route. I was almost in front of my house when three bigger kids stopped me and started shoving me around, wanting to know if I had made any tips I wanted to share with them. Sam must have heard the commotion. He came out of his house and walked over to me like I was his twin brother and said, 'Hey, pal. You having problems with your friends?' One of the tough guys told him to go back inside and mind his own business, or they'd have to bust him up and teach him a lesson. Those were the famous last words in that lesson, and it was the first time I saw Sam use his arms and feet as weapons for real. He came to my rescue in a big way, and we never mentioned it again. We became instant friends

18

and stayed at each other's side no matter what. When we got a little older, we would go out on double dates, and if one of us was dateless, it didn't last long. The girls liked us, and there was always somebody up for a good time at the last minute."

"Later on, there wasn't much Sam wouldn't do to make a buck. He did the usual dog walking and grass cuffing, but he had a more creative entrepreneurial leaning and started making fake IDs. He had a lot of privacy down in the basement, and he liked to tinker with stuff. He would collect old typewriters and things like that. He picked up a junked copier and an ,old laminating machine, and after he got his driving permit at sixteen, he faked his first ID. He was very good at it, and you had to look awfully hard to see flaws in his work. He would sell fake IDs to underclassmen for ten bucks a pop." Griggs stopped to chuckle before continuing with his story.

"Sam was rolling in dough, but he had to be careful since his dad was a cop. We were in our final year of high school and had applied to several colleges. We both got a few acceptance letters back and were trying to decide what to do with the rest of our lives. Graduation was only a couple of weeks away when Sam and I decided to go bar hopping over the weekend. We had heard about a place called Big Bob's that had good country and western bands every Friday night, along with lots of pretty girls who liked to line dance. We decided to see if we could get in."

"Wait!" Clint broke into the story. "You were only seventeen? How did you get into the bars?"

"You haven't forgotten about the fake IDs already, have you? Sam had one, and of course, he had made one for me, too. As long as we stayed out of trouble, we would be all right."

"Getting past the door at Big Bob's was a piece of cake. We were drinking and having a good time, but we knew that since this was our first time there, the bartender was keeping an eye on us. That's when Sam saw this knockout blonde sitting alone at the bar. 'I'm going in for the kill, Jim Boy. Wish me luck,' Sam had said."

"He wandered over in her direction, but before he made it within two feet of her, this big country boy—I mean BIG, six two if he was a foot, and built like a Sherman tank—grabbed the back of his shirt. 'What's on your mind, pardner?' he asked Sam."

"Sam was never one to back down, and maybe it was the beer talking when he answered something like, 'Dancing with this beautiful lady here, pardner. Now step aside.' The plowboy frowned. 'Sorry, pal, but she's with me.' Sam egged him on, 'It's hard to believe she would go out with someone as ugly as you.'

"That's when I knew Sam had just crossed over that line of no return."

"Who was he, the guy?" Clint asked.

"Nobody, really. Just her boyfriend. To make a long story short, Sam tried to hit this country dude, and all you could hear was bones cracking. It sounded like Sam broke every finger in his hand. I stepped over to help him out, and that's when the guy's friends started beating the living daylights out of us. I took a blow in the gut and lost my breath. As I was heading for the floor and my lights started going out, I saw Sam's body kicking and spinning like crazy. Stuff was flying everywhere. Before the cops arrived, Sam picked me up and carried me out of there. Don't ask me what happened to that bartender we were out to impress with our good behavior. He was probably hiding behind the bar. The next morning, I had two slits for eyes and a big hammering headache. My dad had the radio on, and my ears perked up when they mentioned Big Bob's. They were talking about a hurricane hitting Big Bob's that left nothing standing.

"During the fight, my shirt got ripped half off me, and my ID had fallen out. The police paid both Sam and me a visit and arrested us the next day. Sam took most of the heat for starting the fight and damaging property, but the most serious charge was him making those fake ID cards. They said he was contributing to the delinquency of and endangering the lives of minors. Sam's an honest guy, and when he 'fessed up to making and selling them for profit, things got a little stickier.

"Of course, Sam's dad being NYPD didn't make it any easier, or maybe it did. He must have somehow got a word in or pulled in a favor with his neighbor down the block, the judge, and Sam got an unheard of choice of either jail time or the military. He enlisted in the army, and I got two years of probation."

"Wow! So Sam Rufus got the name 'Hurricane' from that bar fight?" Clint asked.

"Yes. After they arrested us, they put Sam's picture and name in the newspaper with the headline 'Big Bob's Hurricane Arrested.' That name has followed him ever since."

Jim went on to tell Clint about how his whole family originally thought Sam's parents were an odd pairing. "Arthur was a hulk, and Anna was a hummingbird. Without exaggerating, Arthur made four of her!"

When they first moved in, Jim's mother had taken them an apple pie as a welcome gift. The next day around suppertime, Sam's mother had returned the kindness with a dish made with corn and seasoned with dried chili peppers. Jim's family had never eaten anything like it. It tasted good, but the hot peppers had set them all on edge for a few days. From then on out, their mothers enjoyed sharing cooking ideas back and forth, but when Arthur decided to put his Italian stamp on the kitchen, things got real interesting.

Anna's heart was as big as her giant husband's. Often, when Jim got together with Sam in the early evening, she would have a big plate of homemade spaghetti and a meatball for him. He would eat until he had to loosen his belt.

"It broke Anna's heart at first when they arrested us, but her real fear was Sam going to jail. What a relief it was for her when Sam chose the service. There had been father-son talks, many of them long after she had gone to bed, and she understood that the decision not only protected him concerning future employment, but it also kept the family name clean."

"Did he serve a full term, or did he get out early?" Clint asked.

"Surprisingly, Clint, or maybe not, Sam served six full years and, in that time, became a Green Beret. That's a pretty unheard of rise, from what I understand."

"I've heard of the Green Berets, and I think, like a lot of people, I'm in awe of them without knowing a whole lot about them."

"I know what you mean. They're supposed to be the best of the best, the select few who really are out there far above and beyond the rest of us when it comes to mental and physical strength and agility. That's where Sam's early martial arts training really took off, and I think it's fair to say, that's where he made himself into the machine he is today. He told me a lot about it in letters during his early training before he started going on actual missions. I think it was a Trojan Warrior program he was in, something like that. He talked about their goals of maintaining this already other-worldly level of physical fitness, then working on improving their weaknesses, then improving themselves as a team. The martial arts part of it had these "S factors." I think it was speed, strength, stamina, stability, suppleness, psychology. Stuff like that. I can't remember them all. And each one of those was broken down into a complex set of components. When they worked on strength, it was about developing maximum strength, explosive strength, speed endurance, muscle endurance, all that. They got into degrees of suppleness like flexibility, mobility, agility and so forth. They worked on aggression, motivation, ambition, expectations, fatigue, energy demands. It was mind-boggling, but he was digging it, and he was getting it. It was singing to him. It all sounded fascinating and over the top, but now all of it is wrapped up inside of him like a wad of rubber bands, and he's one of the most amazing and scary people I know."

"Scary? Why is that, Jim?"

"I'll say only this: be glad he's on our side. I wouldn't want to go up against him one-on-one, or even twenty-on-one. Now, let's get back to work. It's almost daylight, and we have another dead body."

Jim, Clint, and Agent Johnson got back to the business of looking hard for evidence that hadn't surfaced, trying to see some sort of pattern they were missing, anything to move them closer to capture and conviction. They looked at the pins on the map showing where the string of murders had taken place. Nothing made sense there, no reason they could see that Staten Island should be targeted. It was most incredible that nobody had witnessed a killing. Or maybe someone had, but they were too scared to say anything. Who knew? What they did know was that whoever was pulling the trigger didn't care who they killed—man, woman, or child.

"What time is it, Clint?" Jim asked.

"It's almost five-thirty and the start of a brand new day."

"It's time then."

"Time for what?" Clint asked.

"It's time to call Sam."

"Right now? You don't really mean to call him right now, do you?"

"It's probably the only time I'll catch him home, if he hasn't left already." He found Sam's phone number and dialed.

"It's been a while since I talked to him. I hope he hasn't changed his number," Sheriff Griggs said, counting the rings out loud. "Four, five, six."

Chapter Three

The seventh ring snapped Sam from his thoughts. He turned his back on the Manhattan skyline and grabbed the phone. "Rufus," he thundered into the phone.

"Sam, Sam is that you?" Jim Griggs asked.

"Depends on who's asking. Who are you?"

"Sam, it's me, Jim. Can you talk?"

"Jim? Is that you? Sure, I can talk," Sam said. "It's good to hear from you, bud, and given the gravity of how crazy that whole killing spree is over there, I'm surprised you didn't call days ago and in the middle of the night to boot."

"Well, you know I'm not the only one running the show, and I'm sorry to call so early, but I wanted to make sure I reached you. We need to talk," Jim said.

"No need to beat around the bush. I'd have to be deaf, dumb, and blind not to know what you're talking about. It's not just your problem you know, Jim. It's everyone's problem now."

"Thanks, Sam. You may not have heard the latest. We just took another hit around 2:00 this morning. Number eight, female, Caucasian, mid-40s, right through the screen of her kitchen window. Went downstairs to get some milk to take her pills and ka-boom, she's gone. Like somebody was sitting there waiting for her, depending on her to not be able to sleep, to forget something, to flip on a light in a quiet night. Whoever has been doing this has been killing in broad daylight, and nobody sees anything. Now they are going dark."

"Do you think it's 'they'? Maybe it's only one person, and most likely it is," Sam said.

"Maybe, I don't know. I just don't get how so many people can get blown away and there be so few clues. It's making me crazy. How come you're not in on this?" Jim asked.

"It beats me. I've been asking myself the same question. I was just getting ready to head in and talk to the chief about the same thing. It's obvious you could use some specialized help, and I'm clueless why he's got me dickin' around on other stuff while your citizens are being shot to smithereens. I'll try to get over there mid-morning. Is that okay with you?"

"Yup, that'll be fine. Thanks, Sam. We definitely could use someone with your expertise helping us. Is there anything special we can do before you get here?"

"What do you have concerning connections between all the victims? It's got to be something, and that's probably the key we'll need to be able to head 'em off at the next pass, providing there is one. They're pushing their luck."

"We're looking into it, of course, trying to connect the dots. There's nothing concrete yet. Are you thinking these could be planned hits, and not just random?"

"I'm saying probably, or possibly. Either way, we have to check every possibility, no matter how strange it might sound. We might get lucky and uncover a clue we never knew existed, but you know that drill. You've been at this long enough."

"All right. We'll dig deeper after breakfast. That's where we're headed now. Feels like we've got half a day in already."

"I'll be looking forward to seeing you again. It's been way too long. After this is over, old buddy, you'll owe me a steak dinner."

"After this is over and we find and stop whoever is doing the killing, I just might buy you the whole cow!"

"That sounds even better. I'll see you later this morning. Get yourself some grub. By the way, Jim, you said 'we'. Who else do you have investigating over there?"

"NYPD, of course, most of my unit, FBI's Bob Johnson and eight of his men, and we'll probably call the U.S. Marshalls in today. We've been trying to keep hysteria in check by not filling the sidewalks with riflemen and the Guard, but that's obviously not working. When people wake up this morning and hear about the latest shooting, we're going to have to pull out all the stops."

"Got that, and, by the way, Johnson is a good man. I'll see you later," Sam said and hung up.

Outside in the early light, a keen-eyed man on a mission walked a second loop around Sunset Park. He stooped and pushed his way into the vegetation diagonally across the street from the sheriff's department. A ray of sun momentarily flashed on a Winchester rifle he had modified. It had a hair trigger so that when he moved the lever action, the weapon would automatically discharge a bullet. He could send out all six shots in a rapid-fire advantage without pulling the trigger more than once. He had already proven himself an excellent shot. Now he hung low, angled to the building's front door, with his gun pointed and ready to fire.

This hit should come as a complete surprise and send them all reeling worse than they already were. And, for him, it meant a double purse for bagging a lawman, especially this lawman. Clint Jones had made the arrest that started this big ball rolling in the first place, but nobody would figure that out for a while yet. Eight down and this one to go before he was out of there, out of Staten Island anyway. There would be bigger fish to fry.

The three-story, red brick building that housed the department's finance division, detective bureau, and civil court faced Sunset Park at an angle. Like many other buildings in the area, it was old, angular, and utilitarian. A set of double doors opened into a waiting room where hundreds of daily visitors went through metal detectors and waited to be seen and heard on a variety of issues from divorce to driving recklessly. It was toward these doors that Jim Griggs and Clint Jones made their way down the hydraulic elevator in search of breakfast.

Sheriff Griggs stared at the floor numbers in the elevator. He had a load of problems on his mind, as usual, but nothing in his career had been as disturbing as those pressing down on his community at this very moment.

"Jim, I was wondering how you were able to talk Hurricane into joining us," Clint asked, shaking Jim on the elbow.

"Well, I haven't exactly, just yet, but he's well aware of what's going on and will plan to join us sometime mid-morning to talk about it. He's got things to get in line on his end."

"That's great, but how are you going to talk him into it?"

"I don't think I'll have much talking to do, frankly, but I'm quite sure something like this will have to be on his terms."

"Say what? His own terms? From what I've read and heard about him, he'll tear up Staten Island."

"If that's what it takes to stop this madness, what's wrong with that? Jim asked.

"He could stir up a big hornet's nest."

"Hell, what do you think we're living in, Jones? Maybe he'll be able to find who we can't. I've got to believe that, or I would never have picked up the phone."

The elevator stopped on the ground floor.

Clint was quiet for a few seconds, then said, "What about the FBI? How are you going to convince them about Sam taking over?"

"If Sam knows them like I think he probably does, I think he'll be able to work something out with them. We're just going to have to get over all the rank-pulling jurisdiction crap and get down to business. Like Sam said, it's everybody's problem now. Sam is no island. Even though he would probably rather work alone, he's more connected than we could ever dream of being."

"It's six o'clock, and I'm starving. Let's head over to Stella's. We have a long day ahead of us," Jim said.

The double doors opened, and a warm June breeze met them. "Whew, it will be a blast furnace by noon," Clint said.

Shots rang out like a string of firecrackers. Both men hit the ground. Clint was hit in the hand, and looked toward the sound, thinking he caught sight of movement. He returned shots in the direction of the park. There was no further fire. Jim was down. Clint grabbed the two-way from his belt and called for backup and an ambulance.

It looked like Jim had been hit badly. One bullet had torn into his right arm, and there was a second wound in his chest. Dark blood soaked his white shirt, spreading quickly and dripping onto the sidewalk. Clint scrambled to his knees and bent over near Jim's face talking to him calmly and clearly, applying light but even pressure to the area with one bare hand over the other and choking back his panic.

Jim's eyelids fluttered as he attempted to focus.

"Jim, Jim. Look at me. You've been hit. An ambulance is on the way. I'm staying with you, buddy."

A few minutes felt like hours before two ambulances pulled up to the scene. Clint's hands were covered in blood from Jim's wound and his own. After the paramedics stabilized Jim the best they could, they loaded him into the ambulance. Clint asked them how it looked, and when they gave him a blank look and went about their business, he took it to mean not well. A paramedic quickly tended to his hand and loaded him into the other ambulance against his protest of wanting to stay with Jim. Both vehicles activated their sirens and headed toward the hospital.

Clint felt weak from the sight of so much blood, and shock started closing in on him. The paramedic kept close watch on his vitals while assuring him that both he and Jim would be in good hands at Sea View Hospital. They had the best doctors in New York.

Chapter Four

S am stacked the newspapers, turned on the tube to watch the seven o'clock news, and headed to the shower. He would catch the bureau chief in an hour, finish up some paperwork, and head over to see Jim.

They had never worked directly together on much of anything before, much less something of this magnitude. Jim was taking a lot of flack from his borough, his county—hell, all of New York City and the entire country for that matter—for coming up dry on the murders. If there was one person outside his immediate family that Sam wanted to help, needed to help, and probably owed his life to, it was Jim.

Beyond the boyhood antics and the occasional close calls, there was a time when Jim had indeed saved his life. The initial rush of cold water from the shower brought it back, as it always did.

They had both received hockey skates for Christmas and had skated throughout the winter at Central Park. Spring was still a good ways off when the neighborhood twins invited them along for a weekend with their father at their place in the country. It was nothing fancy. A small farm with a cabin, a few fallen-down outbuildings to explore, a garden spot, and a pond perfect for skating. The twins' father had gone to the pond with the boys, and with two shovels between the five of them, they had cleared a sizeable place to skate. The boys played ice hockey using makeshift hockey sticks and river rocks for pucks. It was Jim from across the pond who had heard the cracking ice and saw Sam disappear in the same instant. And it was Jim who did not hesitate to shout orders at the other boys for one to lay down and the other to stand and hold him by the legs as he approached the hole on his stomach like a ladder and reached for Sam's flailing arms. Sam shuddered at the memory and stepped out of the shower.

He dried his thick dark hair first while dripping and moving toward the television. He swiped the bath towel over his well-toned limbs, then stopped in front of the television to see some breaking news. It was the female victim Jim had told him of, whose name was not being released yet, but then … "Moments ago, at approximately six o'clock, Sheriff Jim Griggs and Deputy Clint Jones of the Richmond County Sheriff's Department came under fire and were wounded outside their office in Staten Island. Shots were returned, but there is no information regarding a suspect. Both Griggs and Jones were rushed to Sea View Hospital. Deputy Jones sustained a bullet wound to the hand and is expected to make a full recovery. Sheriff Griggs was wounded in the chest, and his condition is not fully known at this time. We're live outside …"

Sam threw his clothes on, called the elevator and waited while the blood boiled in his veins. Through the lobby and past the doorman, he dashed into the street and hailed the first cab he saw. "Hey, buddy, get me to Whitehall Street to the ferry terminal, and hurry."

The cabbie drove through the streets stopping for nothing or no one except occasional red lights, which he had a knack of avoiding. Sam tipped him heavily, got his ferry ticket and tried to remain calm on the twenty-minute ride. He stood bracing into the wind, seeing nothing but moving images of Jim and himself as boys growing up together, reliving again the memories as they flooded in. Who knows how things might have turned out if Jim hadn't needed a little help protecting his paper route tips that morning so long ago? He drifted back to the heat of that morning as if he had never left. He saw the three punks, heard them chiding Jim, and felt the dizzying thrill of landing his spin kicks. Sam's trance was broken by the boat's nudge against the dock and a press of bodies moving past him to exit.

Sam hailed another cab, and in a few minutes he would be at the hospital. There had been no live news on the ferry, but it was just as well that he was left with his own thoughts, as he was again now.

Sam ordered the cab to the emergency entrance where he showed his badge, inquired about the status and whereabouts of Sheriff Jim Griggs, and was directed to a surgical waiting area.

Jim's wife, Nancy, paced in the open area outside the waiting area. He startled her when he called her name, but when she turned and saw it was Sam, she ran to him and held on for dear life.

"Sam, I don't know what to do. I would be lost without Jim."

"Settle down, Nancy. Jim's a fighter. He will pull out of this."

"Sam, you don't know how bad he is. They're in there right now trying to remove two bullets. One missed his heart by two inches—maybe less. They're talking about maybe a fifty-fifty chance of him pulling through. If he makes if off the operating table, he's heading for ICU."

Nancy was at home when she got the call. She had called her mother to stay with the children and asked her to try to keep the news from them until more was known. Then she raced to the hospital.

She was wild with her own fear, then caught sight of the fire rising in Sam's eyes as he processed the severity of Jim's condition.

"Sam, please don't go out there and get yourself killed, too."

Sam talked with Nancy for a while, asked her if the kids knew yet, and if there was anything she needed. He spent a few minutes reminding her that Jim needed her to think positive thoughts about his recovery. He went to the nurses' station and inquired about the ICU phone number and its waiting room number. "I'll call you a little later to find out how Jim's doing. I should have been here sooner."

"Sam, there would have been nothing you could have done, and maybe both of you would be lying in there. It will be hard enough if I lose Jim, but I would really fall to pieces if both of you died."

"Nancy, nobody is dead yet. Jim's a fighter, and he will do everything he can to pull through. Keep the faith, and I will check back with you as soon as I can."

He turned and walked toward the elevator thinking about the first time

Jim had mentioned a woman named Nancy. It was another one of those "I knew we were made for each other right from the start" moments. Or was it the moment he laid eyes on her, or the moment she first said hello? It was one or all of them. It didn't matter. Sam had been glad for him, and figured they had dated enough ladies to know when the right one was standing in front of them. Sam was best man at their wedding, all the while thinking that it would take Jim a while to forgive him for the 24 rolls of toilet paper he had decorated his car with for the occasion. Removing it had been a problem and had delayed the honeymoon by almost two hours. Sam, of course, maintained that it would have taken a lot less time had it not rained during the reception.

Sam snapped back to the present, pressed the elevator call button and stormed through the opening elevator doors. Clint Jones thought he had been hit in the chest by an armored truck when they collided. "Hurricane?" he ventured, "I'm Deputy Clint Jones, and I'd like to help you."

Hurricane looked at the three-hundred-pound-six-footer with the bandaged hand. He had never met or heard of Clint Jones before but immediately understood his grief, his guilt, and his desire to help.

Still, Sam said, "No, Clint. You and Jim have had enough of this guy. I'm glad you're all right, but a whole lot of other people aren't, and Jim could be dead tomorrow. He called me for help this morning, and I'm here. It's time for an eye for an eye."

"Are you heading over to our office?

Sam nodded, not saying a word.

"How did you get here, taxi?"

Another nod.

"Let me at least drive you there," Clint said. "It will save you time, and I can get you settled in and up to speed so you can get a plan going. Then I'll let you take these keys so you've got something to move around in." He dangled the keys and pressed the Ground button of the buzzing elevator.

Sam nodded something like thanks as the doors closed behind them.

"How did you know who I was?" Sam asked.

"Are you kidding me? I read the papers, every day, and I've seen your picture in so many of them, it's like, duh, how could I not know. Besides Jim told me to look for a guy that moved like a force of nature, and I see he wasn't exaggerating," Clint smiled.

"Clint, there is something you can do for me."

"Just name it, and I'll do anything to help," Clint replied.

"First of all, stay as close to Nancy and Jim as you can until this whole thing is over, and see if you can spare a couple officers to keep an eye on their kids. I know what you're going through and how badly you want to help, but with a busted hand, you're much safer out of the line of fire for now. Besides, when the two of you became targets and with Jim now hanging on by a thread, this got very personal for me. Whoever is out there doing this will pay immensely for their crime, and I don't particularly want you in the line of fire again. But I'm puzzled about something."

"What's that?" Clint asked.

"Jim said, and things certainly point in that direction, that the killer was a sharpshooter. All of the killed have been brought down with a single bullet to the chest, with no other body wounds or signs of multiple, errant shots. The news said at least five or six shots were fired. If that's the case, why would he have fired so many this time?"

"Now that you mention it, I remember Jim pushing me and reaching for his gun just before I heard the first shot. I felt a sting around my belt," Clint said. He remembered his hand was in front of his body. He checked his belt, and there on his holster was a scrape. The bullet could have ricocheted off his gun and into his hand.

Sam saw Clint's face piecing together the events. "Consider yourself lucky that you're left handed. If that holster was on the other side, you might be sharing the bed next to Jim. I think maybe Jim spotted the guy before he fired his gun and that his first shot was for you. It must have careened off your gun, passed through your hand, and hit Jim in the arm. Then, when Jim tried to return a few shots, he was hit near the heart. All this is just conjecture, you know."

"Why would he try and kill us though, Sam?"

"Maybe he was getting paranoid and felt he needed to throw the investigation off track, slow things down on your end, divert your attention from the others in a big way. He may not realize the fire power he's bringing down upon himself. Either he's a cold-blooded butcher, or he's getting crazy and delusional at this point. Whatever he is, he's in more trouble than he could ever have imagined. He's made the Hurricane mad!"

Chapter Five

Sam and Clint arrived at the sheriff's office to see the area still taped off and sidewalk cleanup by a hazmat team underway. They went around to the back door. Reporters hovered for breaking news. Inside the office, deputies and staff were on high alert and speculated among themselves about the man at Clint's side.

Clint led Sam into Jim's vacant office. The two held an animated conversation with hands flying. Clint left and returned shortly with a stack of reports.

Sam studied them for a while, meticulously starting at the top, soaking up words, maps, and photographs at lightning speed, and then neatly placing them face down on the desk. When he finished, he summoned Clint, and in a few words, let him know he would be setting out on his own to hit the streets. He would be back when he found what he needed.

Sam drove to the locations of the different killings and checked in great detail every square inch of the crime scenes and surrounding areas, including the most recent one at the sheriff's office. He was on the streets for three solid days and nights, watching, listening, and piecing together clues and components. He did not shave or change clothes. He drank coffee, ate minimally, and grabbed a few winks in the unmarked patrol car when he needed to. He kept his phone off except to call ICU every few hours to inquire about Jim's condition. Jim made it through surgery, but there had been no change since then, and at the end of each call, Hurricane felt rage and menace rising up in him. He was mad enough to blow a hole through anything or anyone.

Exhaustion started setting in, and knowing he needed rest, Sam went home to a stack of newspapers outside his door and a full voice-message box. Hadley, his chief, was all over him. Where the hell was he, and why wasn't he returning calls? He showered, fell on his bed, and slept. When he awoke, he sensed that something had shifted. He telephoned Nancy at the hospital. He was right. Jim had slipped into a coma.

Sam mumbled some attempt at encouragement to Nancy, and when he hung up, there no longer was a question of how to find and deal with the killer on the loose. Jim had saved his life, and he knew that now it was his turn to repay the favor.

He headed back to the sheriff's office. Deputy Jones was sitting at a desk in the bullpen.

"Clint! What are you doing here?"

Sam's unexpected booming voice made Clint jump. "Sorry, Hurricane, I just couldn't stay home and do nothing without trying to help Jim."

"I guess if I were in your shoes, I would do the same," Sam said. "What have you found out in the past few days that helps makes sense of this?"

"Something is just materializing that's either earth shattering or a total nothing. We're not done yet, but it's looking more and more like a pattern may be emerging," Clint said.

Just as he was about to explain, Agent Johnson pushed the doors open trailed by his agents. "What the hell is going on in here now without our knowledge?"

"Well, hello there, Agent Johnson. It's nice to see you again as well."

"Hurricane, what brings you over on this side of New York? Need I ask? Never mind. I take that back. It's a stupid question," Johnson said.

"Jim Griggs called and asked for my help just before he stepped outside and got himself shot. I wish he had called a day or two earlier. He thought maybe I could shed a little more light on this killing spree."

"When did you get here?" Johnson asked.

36

"About three days ago."

"Three days, and this is the first time we've seen each other? Where have you been?"

"Out and about. I've gone over each of the crime scenes with a fine-toothed comb hoping to find something, anything that may have been overlooked," Sam answered.

"Well? Did you find anything?" Johnson asked.

"Things are picked pretty clean. You guys did a good job as usual. However, there were a few areas I wanted to check again. A couple of the places were still taped off, which surprised me.

"Something came to me, though, with all of the beautification projects in the parks and greenways. When they planted the new bushes and trees, they made a big deal about how they were boating over loads of lime and black dirt to break up the hard soil. They were planning to till the soil and mix it in good before they planted. There are two places in those park projects from where the killer would have struck. The vegetation would have concealed him, and there were signs of disturbance—broken twigs, and so forth. I'm sure you saw those. There were also footprints in those bushes, footprints that wouldn't be from the initial planting, and footprints in places that wouldn't make sense for ordinary maintenance or park visitors. There were some from the park over there across the street and another from the second crime scene. Whether they'll make any sense or turn out to be related, I don't know, but I made some molds, thinking we could take a closer look. The molds are out in the trunk. Would you like the honors, Agent Johnson?"

"It would be my pleasure. Thank you, Hurricane."

Back in the office, after Sam retrieved the cardboard boxes containing the molds and handed them over to Agent Johnson, he turned to Clint and addressed the group of agents. "Clint was just about to give us some information the department is looking at about a possible pattern or a link to a motive. They are still in the process of checking out what he thinks might be important. I think we should listen to him."

"Go ahead Clint. If you have any hunches or information, regardless of how trivial you think it might be, please let us in on it. It's got to add up to more than what we have now," Agent Johnson said.

"Well, you know the hours we've all spent turning over every rock we could find on record and doing extensive interviews with the families of the victims," Clint said. "We're always digging deep for reasons why a killer kills who he kills, especially when he's an expert shot like this one. He's not stealing anyone's wallet or car in the process. Nobody's wife is running off to Mexico with him, and these aren't drug deals gone bad. This guy is doing it for hire, we're pretty sure. Like Hurricane said, we're not finished yet, but a common thread came up in two interviews that sent us packing for court docs. We're reviewing them now."

"Court documents?" Agent Johnson asked. "What kind of court docs?"

"You know how it is when you run the checks and the victim is clean. We get under the skin of the close family about knowing anyone who would have reason to cause them harm. Most times, we come up dry. When we probed further about these victims being witnesses to a crime or an accident, or even serving jury duty in the last five years or so, we came up with two, so far, who were jurors in a domestic violence/assault case that turned real ugly. We thought it was worth checking out and got a hell of a surprise. The guy had been battering his wife for years and then started getting violent with his own kids. When he broke the little boy's arm, the wife filed for divorce, but not before the husband pulled a gun on her. Somehow she calmed him down enough to keep her life and then filed a truckload of assault and battery charges against him, including two assaults with a deadly weapon. She had kept notes on a personal planner of all the times he came after her. Thing is, though, she said she wanted out, but when he begged and cried for forgiveness, she would give him one last chance, even after he had pulled a gun on her the first time. But when he laid a hand on the kid and busted his arm, she was done with him for good. He had whined and pleaded for another chance, but when she told him no and called the cops, he threatened to kill her. I should know. It was me and Deputy Riley who arrived at the scene and took him into custody. He had threatened to kill all of them, and he was still waving a gun at her and both kids when we showed up. It was tense, getting him to put it down.

"Can you believe he pleaded innocent? But the judge admitted the calendar as evidence, and plenty of witnesses showed up. The kids didn't have to rat on their old man. The jury was unanimous in their findings. Guilty. The judge sentenced him to eight years in prison, and as soon as he was behind bars, his wife and the kids disappeared."

"How long ago was that?" Hurricane asked.

"Right around three years ago. I just saw where the guy started serving his sentence on June 15, three years ago."

"What's his name?" Johnson asked.

"Sidney Wallace. He's still in the clink where he belongs," Clint said.

"How many people were on the jury?" Hurricane asked.

"Twelve. A criminal case," Clint answered. "Five of the jurors were from right here in Staten Island, and if it turns out we're right, four of them are dead now, including one of their spouses and two children taken down at the same time. Plus, I'm more convinced than ever that the bullet Jim Griggs took was meant for me. I was the one who cuffed him and humiliated him with his kids and the neighbors looking on."

Sam jumped in. "Good work, Clint. It's not too far fetched to think that this guy could be operating from jail and that he's not just out for revenge against the jurors and you, but he's out to destroy everybody related to his trial. He may or may not be the guy we're ultimately after, but he's worth taking a look at."

"But if he's in prison, you can't link him to the murders, can you? Where's the evidence?" Clint asked.

"Unless, he's connected either on the inside or the outside and compensating someone somehow to kill these people," Johnson said. "Thing is, we've got to figure something out before the next hit comes down. Have you checked out where the other jury members are? We need to identify who else was involved in this case that he could be after, other targets even remotely involved. Let's think about what else we need to consider before going off half-cocked on this. Any ideas?"

Hurricane had listened to it all. He started getting a feeling in his gut, and his gut instincts had never let him down. He just needed a little more information.

"Clint, is there anything big happening in the next few days in the area?" he asked.

"Let me think. I know there's a hospital fundraiser for a new psych wing. The mayor is giving a speech to the students at the Richmond Campus tomorrow night about a shelter project they're taking on. There is a groundbreaking for a new luxury hotel. Gotta keep the tourists coming, you know. Those are the first things to come to mind. Let me get some more people on it."

"Thanks, that's good for now. Let's have a word together," Hurricane said moving in the direction of Jim's office.

"I've got an idea, and it's coming on strong. I'm not going to talk it over with you now, but I'd like to ask you once again to stay out of the line of fire. Wear your bulletproof vest at all times. And stay close to Jim and Nancy's kids. I'll let you know when this is over."

Clint tapped his chest, indicating his vest was on. "Jim told me you have done so much for him that it would take a lifetime to pay you back. This is the least I can do."

"There's not a better friend to be found than Jim Griggs. Now, go on. I'll see you when it's over." Hurricane was ready to leave.

"Hey, Agent Johnson, are you ready to find this creep?"

"Let's go take him down, Hurricane. I've dreamed about saying those few words," Johnson said.

"Okay! I just told Clint I've got a feeling, and they have not let me down yet. Tomorrow night the mayor's going to speak outside at the campus across from the park. I'd like you to send four of your men over to the campus in the mid-afternoon. Have them in plain clothes, ordinary citizens walking around, hanging out, that sort of thing. Have them over by the amphitheater watching the sound set-up and all that. Have two more of your guys covering the eastern approach to the campus, two on the west, and you and I will be in the park. That should cover our bases. If any of your men see anything or anybody unusual or skittish, have them contact you, and then you head over and check them out."

"What if there's no time to get to me?" Agent Johnson asked.

"If that's the case, and there's no doubt that somebody is going down, order your men to shoot to kill," Hurricane said.

"Hurricane, I'm a federal agent, I can't just kill a man without first exhausting other methods to bring him to justice."

"That's fine, Agent Johnson. I've said what I have to say. If you are not up to this, go do your own thing and see if it works any better than what you've been doing. Instead of exhausting other methods, let's talk about methods and justice for the people in the morgue right now, and how Jim might be joining them at any time. If you want to pussyfoot over rules and regulations, go ahead. But for me, that changed the day Jim got shot."

Agent Johnson nodded and, along with his men, exited the building.

Hurricane's patience was growing thin. The next evening had arrived, and the assumptions he was making and his gut feelings were guiding him like a compass. He had acquainted himself with the campus layout earlier in the day and had found a place in the park from which he could see the stage being erected where the mayor would speak. He would be somewhat obstructed by vegetation, but not completely. He settled down for what he hoped would be the end of a long few days.

He looked at his watch and then caught Agent Johnson in his peripheral vision taking a seat on a park bench to read a newspaper. It was nearly six o'clock, and the mayor was due in another half hour. A few people were starting to make their way to the campus. When the sun popped back out from behind the clouds, Hurricane saw a slight flash from the corner of the bleachers. He took out a small pair of binoculars and looked toward the bushes that were almost a block away. Nothing, he saw nothing. It could have been a soda can or a car mirror, but the height had been wrong for both, now that he thought about it. He tried to signal Agent Johnson, but he seemed engrossed in his paper.

Hurricane decided to take a closer look. Dressed in Bermuda shorts, running shoes, and a loose-fitting shirt to conceal his double-packed shoulder holster, he started a slow jog down the block.

Agent Johnson finally saw Hurricane, and when he looked in the direction he was going, he knew something was about to happen. When Hurricane was a little more than half way to the corner, a car pulled up across the street. "Oh, hell, it's the mayor." He started to run while reaching inside his shirt for his two .357 Magnums just as the barrel of the rifle was raised to fire.

"No! Get down!" Hurricane yelled, as a shot rang out. The shooter came into view, and when he saw Hurricane coming at him, he leveled his gun at Hurricane's chest and pulled the hair trigger.

Hurricane couldn't believe how fast the rifle was firing. He hadn't hit the deck that fast since his service days. He took quick but steady aim and fired both his guns. As the first rounds hit their target, the shooter slowly folded to the ground, but still held on to his weapon.

Hurricane yelled, "Drop your gun!" When he didn't respond, Hurricane thought about Jim and the other victims as he pumped all twelve rounds into him, yelling, "This is for all the others you killed, and for Jim and Clint."

By the time Agent Johnson made it over to the scene, the shooting was over, and the shooter lay in a bloody pile. Hurricane ran over to check on the mayor. His arm had been grazed, but he was all right.

Hurricane walked back to the scene as Agent Johnson was bagging a rubber-banded wad of money, a set of keys, and a list that had been blown from the shooter's pocket. "Hang on to that for a while, and get this scene under control, will you? I've got someplace to go and will catch up with you later."

It had been hours in the making, but Hurricane believed his job was over for the moment. He felt certain they had gotten their man. He packed his guns back in their holsters, walked away from the scene, and hailed a cab to the hospital.

It was the ICU nurse who informed Sam that Sheriff Jim Griggs had expired that afternoon. He must have stood there looking at her for several minutes before he turned slowly and left the building. He would call Nancy in the morning, but not right now.

Chapter Six

It had been nearly six months since Sheriff Jim Griggs had been fatally shot. Sam Rufus was sitting in the courtroom awaiting his verdict for killing a man—the murderer who had terrorized Staten Island in a killing frenzy that had included their sheriff, one of his closest friends.

A week after it had happened, a newly-formed group called Urban Citizens against Gun Violence filed charges and made a case that Sam not only used excessive force, but that he was guilty of murder. They figured that one bullet alone could have stopped the murderer, and it had not been necessary for him to unload all twelve rounds into him.

Before the police and ambulance made it to the scene, FBI Agent Johnson and Hurricane had found keys, a hand-written list, and a roll of money next to the killer's body. It would be two days later before Agent Johnson and Hurricane saw each other again. Agent Johnson, at Hurricane's request, had kept the materials from the police. Now, in Jim Grigg's office with the door closed, they both donned latex gloves and dumped the contents from the plastic collection bag on Jim's desk. None of the keys on the generic keyring belonged to a vehicle that might lead to further clues, but fingerprints were a possibility. Johnson counted the money while Hurricane carefully unfolded the bloodied list.

"Hurricane," he whistled, "there's twenty-five grand here."

"Yeah, well, I'm beginning to see how he came up with it. Look at this."

Fifteen names had been scrawled on the paper with a black felt tip pen, and five of them, with $5,000 by each name, were crossed off. That could explain the wad Agent Johnson had just counted, a sort of pay as you go arrangement. Beside some of the names, there was a street address. By others, a word or so about spouse or kids.

"Looks like the piece of dung was checking them off like a grocery list," Hurricane said.

"Are you thinking what I'm thinking, Hurricane?"

"Probably." Sam smoothed out the paper and examined it closer.

"That's them all right."

The names of five Staten Island victims stared back at them. And that wasn't all.

"Okay, things are really hitting the fan now. Here's 'Jones–arrest–$10,000'. And what's this? It looks like 'Grogan–judge–$15,000', and 'Mayor–$15,000'. Bingo! It's a real hit list, all right. What do you think about that?"

Agent Johnson whistled again as he pointed to the names marked $5,000 that weren't crossed off yet. "And what about these three names on the back—Connie, Jimmy, and Shirley?"

"That's got to be Wallace. But how's he doing it?"

Sam had poured over the case records and knew that the three names on the back were Wallace's immediate family, his wife Connie and two children, Jimmy and Shirley. That was easy. He had tried to locate them and found out they were placed into the witness protection program. Finding them now to warn them would be like trying to find a needle in a haystack. Maybe the program was taking good enough care of them. He hoped so. There were concerns about the lives of the other people on the list. For four months, covert surveillance had been placed on each residence but then had stopped as quickly as the deaths in Staten Island.

Time had run out before Sam was able to dig up anything else, and now he was on trial for killing the man who had killed many others. He and Agent Johnson agreed to withhold the list and the money until the trial was over. Sam told his attorney about what they had found, and she, in an unusual move, shared the information with prosecuting attorney Tony Duncan. She had introduced the matter to him slowly at first, using hypothetical scenarios to feel him out. When she felt he was in agreement with her and her client that withholding the list was in the best interest of protecting those on it, she spilled, and he promised to keep the confidence.

Defense attorney Sandy Keller was sitting next to her client re-reading the statement he had given prior to his court date. Sam was physically there like the force he was, but his mind was miles away. A door in the front of the courtroom opened.

"All rise for the Honorable Judge Charles Grogan," the bailiff said.

Everyone stood as the judge seated himself behind his desk. "Be seated," he stated, not looking up. He reviewed the documents before him and pronounced that things were in order. The prosecution began.

"Your Honor, the prosecution calls Amelia Post."

A young woman approached the bench, and raised her right hand, as instructed.

The bailiff said, "Do you promise to tell the truth, the whole truth, and nothing but the truth, so help you God?"

"Yes, I do," Amelia answered.

The prosecuting attorney stood, approached the judge's desk, and said, "Hello, Amelia. My name is Tony Duncan. I represent Urban Citizens against Gun Violence. I understand you were a witness to the events that occurred on June 23 last?"

"Yes, I was there," she said.

"Could you tell us in your own words what you saw on that day?"

"Yes. I finally had a day off from work and decided to take my dog for a walk. By the time I made it to the park, it was about 5:30, or maybe a little later in the afternoon. The sun had just poked out from behind the clouds, and it was blinding for a few minutes. When I looked into the park, I saw a man dart out from behind the bushes and start to run north, very slowly at first. Then I saw a black, sort of official-looking car go by. It was slowing down and pulled up to the curb by the campus. The man who was running started running faster toward it. He took out two guns from under his shirt, and as the man, who turned out to be the mayor, got out of the car, the guy yelled and raised his guns. That's when I heard a shot, and when I looked in the direction of it, I saw a man carrying a canvas bag come out into the open from the bleachers. He had what looked like a short rifle, and he pointed it toward the man running at him, and started to shoot. It sounded like firecrackers going off. Then the man who was running toward him was on his belly on the sidewalk and started shooting his guns, and no matter how many bullets hit the man with the rifle, he held onto it. It looked like he was doing a dance, until he fell to the ground."

"Amelia, can you recall how many shots you heard?"

"I never counted them. I just keep seeing that man holding onto his gun until he stopped dancing."

"Amelia, is the man you saw shoot the victim in this courtroom today?" Tony Duncan asked.

"Yes, he is. He's sitting right there, and I'll never forget his face," Amelia said pointing to Hurricane.

"The prosecution has no other questions for this witness, Your Honor," Tony Duncan said.

"Attorney Keller, do you have any questions for this witness?"

Sandy Keller approached the witness. "Amelia, I'm sorry you had to be a witness to such a brutal scene, but do you think the man you pointed to is a hero or a villain?"

"If he had not shot that man, our mayor would be dead today. How can you not consider him a hero?" Amelia answered.

"Thank you, Amelia. The defense has no other questions for this witness, Your Honor."

Amelia Post was excused, and three more witnesses were brought up to testify. They gave the same story as Amelia.

It was mid-morning by the time Sam was called to take the stand. He approached and raised his right hand.

"Mr. Rufus," the bailiff asked, "do you promise to tell the truth, the whole truth, and nothing but the truth?"

"Yes, I always tell the truth," Sam replied.

"Please state your name for the court."

"Samuel James Rufus."

Sam was told to be seated, and Judge Grogan ordered the prosecuting attorney to begin his cross examination.

"Thank you, Your Honor. Please state your name one more time for me."

"Samuel James Rufus."

"You mean 'Sam Hurricane Rufus,' don't you?" Tony Duncan inquired.

"My legal name is Samuel James Rufus. Hurricane is a nickname."

"How did you get the name 'Hurricane'?" Tony Duncan asked.

"When Sheriff Jim Griggs and I were younger and lived next door to each other, we got into a fight in a bar. During that fight, in which we were out numbered, I employed several martial arts kicks and moves. I started spin kicking so quickly that they called me a hurricane."

"This was in a bar, is that right?" Tony Duncan asked.

"Yes," Hurricane replied.

"And you were under age at the time, is that right?"

Hurricane's attorney jumped up to object to the line of questioning, "This has nothing to do with the shooting, Your Honor."

Tony Duncan said, "Your Honor, this is relevant to the case to let the jury know what kind of person Mr. Rufus is."

Judge Grogan said he would allow the question but warned Duncan not to go too far.

"Now, Mr. Rufus, were you under age when you went into this bar?"

"Yes, I was," Sam answered.

"How did you get into a bar without a proper proof of your age?"

"I made fake identification cards."

"So you are no saint when it comes to breaking the law?"

Sandy Keller objected, stating that the matter happened when Sam was a kid. "We all did stupid things when we were young, things we always regret later, especially if we become important figures in our communities," she said.

"Mr. Duncan, please just get to your point," the judge ordered.

"Yes, Your Honor. Mr. Rufus, where did you learn how to fight with weapons?" Tony Duncan asked.

"I served six years in the army, three of them as a Green Beret," Sam responded.

"Did you receive any jail time for breaking the law and, in a sense, contributing to the delinquency of minors, of which you, yourself, were one?" Tony Duncan asked.

"I was given a choice of four years in prison or six years in the military," Sam answered. "Military service not only taught me how to use weapons, it also taught me how to track down the enemy and use my bare hands against them."

"When you say 'the enemy', Mr. Rufus, who are you referring to?"

"Anyone who breaks the law."

"In other words, if I were to speed past you or steal a candy bar, I become the enemy, and you would have to shoot me?"

Sam answered, "No, those are just little crimes. I'm talking about the thugs who torture and kill people for fun or for pay."

"So you shoot to kill, period?"

"No, the enemy is given two choices: surrender or die," Sam answered.

"So you become judge, jury, and the executioner all in one?"

"In this case, yes. This man killed innocent law-abiding and civic-minded citizens, a spouse, two children, my best friend and your sheriff, Jim Griggs. He wounded Deputy Jones and attempted the life of our mayor. He would have killed him, too, had I not been there. When I started shooting, all I could think about was Jim Griggs' life slipping away from him in the hospital while his wife looked on. I didn't want anyone else to get hurt or die."

"I'm trying to understand what you are telling us, but you are an officer of the law. You should know better," Duncan stated, stealing a glance at the jury.

"I know, but had I wounded him, he may have gotten off another shot at the major or someone else, including myself. He also may have gotten off on a technicality. It happens far too often. He may have ended up back on the street killing more people. Some legal matters would have been messed up or overlooked, and besides, I could have missed him with my first couple of shots," Sam answered.

"The first shot alone almost took his arm off with those cannons you used. That should have been enough to stop him cold. Why did you continue firing your weapon, or weapons in this case, putting all twelve bullets into the victim?" Tony Duncan asked.

"As I said before, I lost my head for a brief instant. When I understood that the mayor was the intended target, I couldn't let another good man get killed for no reason."

"How long have you been on the police force, Mr. Rufus?"

"Five years, going on six."

"How many times have you fired your weapon?"

"I have fired it ten or maybe fifteen times."

"How many of the people you shot at did you kill?"

"Objection, Your Honor," Sandy Keller yelled. "This is irrelevant to the case."

"Overruled," the judge said. "Please answer the question."

"Four, but they were all in self defense," Sam answered.

"Did any of those cases go to court?"

"No. Like I said, they were all clean shots in self defense."

"So, your act of violence is an ongoing thing?" Tony Duncan asked.

"Objection, Your Honor. The prosecution is badgering the witness," Sandy Keller said.

"Objection sustained, the jurors will disregard the prosecutor's last question. Mr. Duncan, you're walking a very fine line," Judge Grogan said.

"The prosecution rests at this time, Your Honor."

Chapter Seven

There was a brief moment of silence before Sandy Keller slowly rose from her chair and approached the stand. "Mr. Rufus, you stated that you had killed four people while on duty, but you weren't asked about the circumstances that prompted you to fire your weapon. Please explain so the jury understands," she asked.

"I was a street cop in my second year when a call came in about a robbery in progress. The perp, a guy named Samuels, fled the scene and was weaving in and out of traffic. The police were in pursuit. I don't really know what happened, but his car started to overheat. He stopped in front of a school and ran inside where about thirty students were having summer school lessons. When the teacher asked him what he was doing, he shot her right in front of her students. By the time we arrived on the scene, he was holding a little girl hostage. He demanded a car, or the girl was going to die. I communicated with my commanding officer who asked me if I had a clean shot. I told him I did, and he ordered me to fire. Even though I told him I only had a head shot, he told me again to take it. We needed to get that teacher some medical assistance fast. So I took the shot, and that is the end of the story."

Sandy Keller asked, "Why would your commanding officer order you to shoot to kill as opposed to wounding him?"

"As I said, I had the shot, he told me to take it, and I did," Hurricane responded.

"Why was he confident you wouldn't hit the little girl?"

"Because I am an expert marksman. I was a sharpshooter in the Berets, along with a couple other guys. We were the best in our unit. Our jobs were to kill our enemies and leave no survivors. There was no way I would have hit the little girl."

Sandy Keller asked, "Do you ever feel remorse after killing someone?"

"All of the time. I always hope and pray that I will not have to kill someone, but unfortunately, sometimes I have to kill somebody to save somebody else."

"Isn't there an easier, or different, approach you can use besides killing someone?" she asked.

"Our commanding officer is very good at negotiating with people, and I've seen him talk people into giving themselves up without a fight. Then there are those who not only pose a threat to themselves, but all the people around them. I would say my commanding officer has talked about 90 to 95 percent of the criminals we face into surrendering. But again, there are those who take hostages and hold them with the threat of killing them. Our commanding officer doesn't much care for that kind, and most of the time, they end up in a bad way. If we can't talk them down and it looks like nobody is going to get hurt, he'll order to shoot to disable. But if there are innocent bystanders or hostages involved and any of them are harmed and need medical care, he will not hesitate to solve the situation as fast as possible, even if it means killing the perpetrator. Lieutenant John Luther gets very upset when innocent people get hurt or killed."

Sandy Keller asked, "So, the only time you have killed anyone came as the result of a direct order?"

Tony Duncan stood up, "Objection, Your Honor, this has no bearing on this case."

Sandy Keller responded, "Your Honor, the prosecution opened up this line of questioning. I'm just trying to establish to the jury that there was a reason my client has killed before."

Judge Grogan said, "I'll allow the questioning. I am also curious as to Mr. Rufus's background. Please answer the question, Mr. Rufus."

"Yes, the only time I have killed was under direct orders."

Sandy Keller asked, "How and why were you involved in the shooting on June 23rd?"

"Sheriff Jim Griggs called me and asked for my help. He understood the level to which I was trained in the Green Berets and that my missions were to seek and destroy. He also knew I have the ability to track, for lack of a better word, a situation quickly given a certain amount of facts, and since he was unable to get a handle on who or what he was looking for, and people were dying every day, he thought I could help him."

"What kind of help was he asking for?" Sandy Keller asked.

"I never had a chance to find out. Before I could get to the department to see him, he had been shot and was in no shape to tell me what he wanted me to do. Since his department hadn't been able to successfully go after this murderer, I decided, with some help from Deputy Jones who provided me with information about their investigation to date, to look into the case on my own, and that's when I found out the FBI was involved. Deputy Jones, because he was injured, was encouraged to devote himself and whatever reasonable resources were available to the safety and protection of Jim Griggs' family. Agent Johnson and I put our heads together and came up with a plan. We narrowed down certain assumptions and suspicions as to where the next strike might take place. I had no intentions whatsoever about going after this guy, unless I was needed, but I had wondered why I wasn't called in sooner," Hurricane said.

"So your initial intent was only as an observer?" Sandy Keller asked.

"Yes," Hurricane answered.

"What happened?" Sandy Keller asked again.

"Jim, Sheriff Griggs, was a day late in asking for my help. Maybe if I had been there, Jim and Deputy Jones might never have been shot. I don't really know if I could have prevented the shooting, but the killer may have been a little reluctant to open fire on three people instead of two, especially lawmen," Sam stated.

"That's a bold statement, Mr. Rufus. Could you please elaborate so the jury and the rest of us can understand what difference your being there might have made?" Sandy Keller asked.

"He used a Winchester, which only holds six shots despite him rigging a hair trigger on it so he could fire in rapid succession if he wanted to. At first, I thought he emptied out his gun, sending all six shots and only hitting his targets with three of his bullets. However, Deputy Jones and I went over the facts. We figured that Sheriff Griggs must have caught a glimpse of the shooter and tried to push Deputy Jones out of the line of fire. One of the bullets careened off of the deputy's gun, first passing through his hand and striking Sheriff Griggs in the arm. Then when the sheriff turned to face the shooter, the other bullet found its mark by his heart. I feel that had I been there, he would not have had time to reload and fire more shots. Therefore, he might never have felt the time was right, and just maybe Jim Griggs would still be alive today. This man was a lot smarter than anyone thought. He had a set of marching orders and a very strategic plan."

"Then how did you know where he would be?" Sandy Keller asked.

"I didn't really know. It was a calculated guess. After reading the clips, going over all the crime scenes and reports, and then hearing Clint Jones' revelation about a domestic violence trial where it seemed like its jurors were being targeted, and then knowing the mayor's sympathetic leaning toward battered women and thinking about the talk he was giving at the campus that night about the women's shelter project, it all just came together in my gut. After the killer exhausted the jurors in Staten Island and tried to take down Clint Jones and Jim Griggs, we figured he might be getting ready for a bigger strike while still in the area. We were lucky the mayor took his time getting out of his car, which gave me enough time to get into position to warn him."

"At what point did you fire your weapon?" she asked.

"His first shot was directed at the mayor, and then he turned toward me and fired. I reacted and sent twelve shots in his direction," Hurricane said.

"So this was self defense?" Sandy Keller asked.

"Yes. And besides, more innocent people may have been shot had I not stopped him."

"Did you know Sheriff Griggs had died before you shot the killer?" she asked.

"No. I had not talked to anyone there since early afternoon, a few hours before the shooting. He had slipped into a coma. I had a feeling he wouldn't pull out of it, but I didn't know he died until after the shooting when I went to the hospital," Sam said.

"What did you do after you learned Sheriff Griggs had died? After you left the hospital, that is," she asked.

"I was wiped out, emotionally drained. I went back to Manhattan and took a long walk past the houses where Jim and I had first met and grown up together. After that, I went to a few bars and toasted my childhood friend and remembered him in my own way," Sam said, his voice softening as he remembered the day.

"I have no further questions."

"Mr. Duncan, do you have any more questions for the defendant?" Judge Grogan asked.

"Yes, Your Honor. I do have a few questions. Thank you."

"Mr. Rufus," Tony Duncan said, slowly walking to the witness stand, "you indicated that this shooting was totally in self defense?"

"Yes."

"Couldn't you have just wounded him?"

"As I said, I was worried about other people and how many more he could have shot had I not stopped him."

"That may be a valid point, indeed, but my question was, could you have wounded him?"

"Yes, I could have, but I was concerned about other people in the immediate proximity at that time."

"You never gave him a chance, did you?" Tony Duncan pushed.

"What kind of chance should I have given him, sir? The chance to complete his mission? The chance to kill innocent bystanders? And what chance did he give the other people he killed. None of them had it coming. They died because they were upstanding citizens doing their duty."

"You appointed yourself executioner, didn't you, Mr. Rufus? You could have shot him only once, couldn't you?" Tony Duncan asked.

"Objection, Your Honor! The prosecutor is badgering the witness!" Sandy Keller stood, her palms resting on the table.

"Mr. Duncan, I hope you're almost done," Judge Grogan said.

"Yes, I am, Your Honor."

"Very well, then. The question stands; objection overruled."

"Should I ask you the question once again, Mr. Rufus?" Duncan asked.

"No, I remember the question," Hurricane responded. "I shot him for every family he ruined and for each person he killed."

Tony Duncan looked around at the jurors and felt he was losing them. He knew he had to do something desperate. They had lapped up everything Hurricane dished out on the stand and had been swayed, too, by his Green Beret uniform and all his medals, including the Medal of Honor, he had noticed. This must have been Sandy Keller's little trick suggestion. He had seen her ask her clients to appear in uniform before, and it usually worked. Now he had to cross a boundary that could get him, Tony Duncan, Esquire, in serious trouble. He felt he had no choice but to take that chance.

"Mr. Rufus, what did you do with the list and the money that were found on the victim?"

Sam was stunned but kept his cool as he saw the fear in Duncan's face and turned to the equally surprised Sandy Keller. His mind was racing about how to best answer the question when Sandy Keller stood up and asked, "Your Honor, I'd like to request a short recess."

"What is the reason for the recess, Attorney Keller?" the judge asked.

"Your Honor, may we discuss this matter in your quarters or approach the bench?"

"You two, please approach the bench," Judge Grogan said.

As they approached, the attorneys were arguing.

"What seems to be the problem here suddenly?"

"Your Honor, the prosecution and I agreed not to disclose this information due to the safety concerns of others," Sandy Keller said.

"Disclose what information?" the judge asked sternly.

"This isn't the place to talk about this, Your Honor," Sam interjected.

"There will be a fifteen minute recess," Judge Grogan said to the courtroom. Then turning to the attorneys and Sam, "You three come into my chambers."

When they were behind closed doors, Sandy Keller started yelling at Tony Duncan.

Judge Grogan raised his hands and the room became quiet. "Now what is going on here with the two of you?"

"We had agreed in advance not to bring the list up in this case today, and this back stabber tried to Pearl Harbor us. Where are your ethics, Duncan?" Sandy Keller demanded.

"What list? Is there something here I don't know about? Somebody, please explain," Judge Grogan asked.

"Your Honor, if I may?" Sam asked. Judge Grogan nodded yes, and Sam continued.

"FBI Agent Johnson and I found a list and twenty-five thousand dollars cash on the victim."

"Why wasn't this reported?"

"It was reported, Your Honor, to a degree. The list was being kept quiet until we had adequate time to thoroughly investigate and prove who is really behind all of this."

"Behind what? What are you talking about?" the judge asked.

"It appears to be a hit list, Your Honor, and we were concerned if word leaked out too far that we had it, the others on that list could be in trouble. As it was, instead of making it public and causing further panic, surveillance protection for every home on the list had been provided, unbeknown to them, for four months. Things were quiet, and the threat had disappeared, or at least it had diminished. The killings had stopped after five people on the list died and attempts were made on two who survived," Sam told him.

"How many names are on the list?" Judge Grogan asked.

"A dozen or more, Your Honor, but the one that bothers us most today, Sir, is yours," Sam said. He produced a copy of the list that he had made and handed it to Judge Grogan.

"My God, my wife and kids are on here. This will not be brought up in this case. Do you hear me, Mr. Duncan? If you so much as breathe a word of this, I will have your license stripped, and you will never practice law in this state again. Do-I-make-my-self-clear?" He emphasized every syllable as he glared at Duncan.

When they re-entered the courtroom and the judge took his seat he asked, "Are there any more questions at this time?"

Tony Duncan announced, "The prosecution rests, Your Honor."

"The defense also rests, Your Honor."

After the jury was escorted from the courtroom, Sam and Sandy sat on a bench in the hallway. A little girl carrying a bag of gummy bears approached them and held out her bag to Sam.

"You want one?" she asked.

Before he could respond, her mother was there with a smaller child in tow. She offered a small smile and an apologetic glance at her daughter as Sam scrambled to remember if he knew them from somewhere. He didn't think so.

"My mommy said you shot the bad man who shot my daddy, and that you're her hero."

There was nothing further the woman needed to add. She and Sam exchanged introductions, and he said to her, "No matter what happens, I'm glad I put that man in the grave. Had he lived, he may have gotten off or gotten out of prison or something and been out shooting more people. This way I know the streets are a little bit safer without him around."

With a nod of agreement from the mother and a bag of gummy bears pushed into Sam's hand, they were gone.

Sandy Keller said not a word, but her elbow lightly brushed his sleeve.

She was a small woman, Sandy Keller, one who could barely stretch to her full height of five feet, but she had other stature as evidenced by an office wall full of awards that trailed the Dean's List at Harvard Law.

"You're like my mother in a way, tough for such a petite lady. I don't know what you think of me personally, but if I had to do it all over again, I'd do it the same way. No matter what happens to me now, I know you gave it your best, and I want to thank you for believing in me."

58

Chapter Eight

The jury took three days to deliberate. Urban Citizens against Gun Violence had filed first and second degree murder charges and a third charge for excessive force with a deadly weapon.

Judge Grogan did not see Sam as a flight risk, so he granted him freedom until they heard the verdict. It was a long three days for Sam. He was told by his attorney, Sandy Keller, that the longer the jury deliberated, the better it looked for him.

"I find this a little ironic," Sam told her. "There were so many times in my adolescent days when Jim and I could have done a little time in the juvie jail system for some of the stunts we pulled. In fact, if not for the influence my father had on others, I could have spent four years in prison instead of six fighting for my country. Now I'm a detective trying to clean up our streets, and for this, I find myself back in court for taking a man off the streets who not only killed several people but changed for the worse so many others in the process. Is this justice when the innocent get punished?"

"Relax, Sam. These jurors have feelings. They are human beings," Sandy Keller said.

Sandy Keller notified Sam on Monday to be in court the next day by ten in the morning. The trial, although not quite on the front page of the paper, had received coverage, so when Sam arrived at 9:30, he was met by a crowd outside the courthouse with signs that read "Unleash the Hurricane" and "We Don't Lock Up Our Heroes." Sam was surprised and a little amused at the visible and vocal support.

Ten o'clock came and with it an absolute silence that filled the room until Judge Grogan entered and was seated.

He addressed the room, "Before I read the verdict, I would like to say that this has been a particularly difficult trial for me. I understand that Mr. Rufus, like all of us, was under a great deal of stress and frustration about the string of murders in our community and particularly that of his good friend and ours, Sheriff Jim Griggs. Still, the law is the law, and despite our own personal traumas, we as citizens must live by the law and a certain set of standards."

There was a slight pause before the judge spoke again, "Jurors, have you reached a verdict?"

The jury captain stood. "Yes, we have, Your Honor."

"May I see it, please?"

The answer was passed to Judge Grogan who read and returned it.

"Will the defendant please rise."

Sandy Keller and Sam rose from their chairs. There were three verdicts to read. Sam looked directly at the members of the jury as the judge asked the questions.

"What say you, jury of the court, with the verdict of first degree murder?" the judge asked.

"Your Honor, we the jury find the defendant, Samuel James Rufus, not guilty," the captain read.

A small "Free the Hurricane" sign, along with an accompanying cheer, went up in the courtroom and was promptly silenced.

"What say you, jury of the court, with the verdict of second degree murder?"

"Your Honor, we the jury find the defendant, Samuel James Rufus, not guilty" the captain read again.

"What say you, jury, on the excessive force that was used in the shooting?"

"Your Honor, we the jury find the defendant, Samuel James Rufus, not guilty due to temporary insanity" the jury captain read.

There was a loud, approving roar and applause after the final verdict was read. Sandy Keller and Sam hugged and shook hands, but Judge Grogan wasn't finished. He pounded his gavel until the room was silent, and then he proceeded.

"Samuel James Rufus, you have been found innocent of all charges. The court, however, recognizes that you have been through a close and personally terrible ordeal and orders you to seek grief and psychological counseling for a thirty-day period to clear your mind. Your right to carry a weapon of any kind during this time is revoked."

After thirty days, we will evaluate your progress and determine if you are mentally stable enough to resume your job and carry a weapon. As of now, you are on a thirty-day suspension with pay until further notice. Thank you, members of the jury. Court is adjourned."

Sam pushed his way through the crowd of reporters and flashing cameras toward a taxi that was waiting for him. He did not acknowledge the dozen microphones being shoved in his face or the questions that were being shouted at him. Sam entered the taxi and looked straight ahead as they pulled away.

Chapter Nine

It had been a grueling six months of depositions, lawyer talk, and opening the Pandora's Box on Sidney Wallace who sat in jail sixty miles away. The Bureau of Prisons had turned over copies of the applications made by all those who wished to visit Wallace in jail, as well as a log of visitors he had seen since he began serving time. It had taken a while to check out the list of approximately twenty. The guy didn't have that many friends and only a brother, another bad seed sitting in another jail whose lousy life was being supported by the taxpayers, for a while yet anyway. The Staten Island shooter had not been traced to Sidney Wallace. Most of the people who had completed visitation applications had backgrounds that were clean, with a couple of exceptions, and the FBI was keeping an eye on them.

The trial was over, he was a free man, and finally Sam had a chance to reflect on what happened to his childhood friend Jim Griggs. It had been an emotional time for him, and it seemed that just when he was starting to get his head back on straight, he was back to square one. "Maybe the counseling will do me some good," he said to himself.

"Hey, Mister Hurricane, are you all right? Or am I at the wrong address?" the cabby asked.

Sam finally realized he was in front of his apartment building. "Thanks, buddy. How much do I owe you?" he asked.

"Nothing. This ride was on me," the cabby said.

"Thank you. If I read your name tag right, it's Joe. Not to sound ungrateful, Joe, and if you don't mind my asking, why the free ride?" Sam asked him.

"One of those guys that madman killed was my brother-in-law, and as far as I'm concerned, you did the right thing," Joe said.

"Thanks, and keep the faith," Sam said and exited.

He was finally alone in his apartment and closed the door behind him with a sigh of relief. A bottle of Jack Daniels stared at him from the antique bar that used to be his father's. He took out a glass and poured. Why not? He could use a good stiff drink, before noon or not. He sank down into the cushions of the couch, and just when the sting hit his lips, there was a knock at his door. It was an insistent knock. *That's odd,* he thought, *the doorman knows better than to let anyone up here without announcing them, and it better not be some sneaky reporter.*

Before Sam opened the door, he went into his closet and retrieved the .44 he kept for special occasions. He looked through the peep hole and saw what looked like the back of a woman's head. Slowly, he turned the doorknob while holding the gun in his other hand and then quickly flung it open wide, scaring the wits out of the woman standing there.

Sam half-apologized, half-threatened, "I hope you're not a reporter, or I'll have your butt thrown out of this building before you can whip your notepad out. Now, how did you get up here, and who are you?"

"Never mind how I got up here, and my name is Carol."

Well, he thought, *she's a little pushy for being on my turf,* but he wondered if there was a little false bravado in her voice, and was trying to figure out if they had met before. She was tanned, which he thought unusual even in this mild winter, and close to six-feet tall. She reminded him of an exotic jungle animal, and the curves beneath her fitted blouse and pants would make a snake jealous. Sam filed his observations, shrugged his shoulders, and said, "Okay, what's up. What are you doing knocking on my door?"

"Doug Stone told me if I was ever in trouble to look you up."

"Doug Stone? Well, I have hardly heard from Doug since he was transferred over to the 67th Precinct in Brooklyn, and that was two years ago. When I was starting out as a detective in Manhattan, it was Doug who took me under his wing, so to speak. He was one great guy, Doug was, easy to get along with even when he was hard at it. We got to be pretty good friends. There's nothing I wouldn't do for him."

He caught himself rambling to this stranger, then inquired, "By the way, how did you find me?"

"Are you kidding me? Your name is plastered all over the papers all the time. A blind person could have found you. When you jumped into that taxi in front of the courthouse, all I had to do was write down the cab company and the license plate number. I went down to the station, told them I was your sister trying to find you, and here I stand."

"How did you know about the taxi?"

"Television. It's a marvelous thing. You have to know there was film coverage of you coming down the steps and pushing through the crowd. Lucky for me there was a perfect shot of the cab and its plate number as it drove off."

Sam wasn't sure he believed her, but got quiet as he wondered how many other people could find him the same way. If Carol was able to track him down so easily and show up at his door in a pretty secure building, maybe he should think about getting away for a while. He snapped back to reality and asked, "I asked you before, why me, why Doug Stone?"

"Two weeks ago," she started as tears clouded her pretty green eyes.

"Wait," Sam said and stepped to the side. "Come in."

"Thank you. Two weeks ago our sixteen-year-old daughter didn't come home from a movie with her friend. My husband drove around the neighborhoods where they had gone to the movies, any place he could think of, trying to think things through. He finally found her car four or five miles from her friend's place. It had a flat tire and was parked across the street from a construction site. It appeared that someone may have stopped and offered to help her, but then took her instead. My husband called me and told me about coming across the car and how he was surprised to see her purse and keys still in it with the doors unlocked. He was looking at the construction site and told me he was going in to have a look around. That was the last I heard from him."

"You contacted the police right away, right?" Sam asked.

"Well, not exactly, not directly. But it wasn't long after he and I talked before they called me saying that my husband had been shot and that he had been able to call in his whereabouts. Somehow the police got over there to the construction site and got him out and to the hospital. He was in pretty bad shape. He was in and out of consciousness for the better part of three days, and then after surgery to remove a bullet, he's started gradually coming around. It's funny, but Doug told me only a few days before he got hurt that if anything ever happened to him, I was supposed to try and contact you."

"All right, so Doug told you if you were in trouble to look me up, and he told you that if anything ever happened to him, to look me up. I'm feeling a little special here, and more than a little surprised. I had no idea he felt that way. How do you know Doug? Do you work with him?"

"Doug Stone is my husband," Carol said.

"Wow! I didn't know Doug was married. When did this happen?"

"We decided to keep it simple and very quiet, only family. I was married once before for nearly ten years and had a child," Carol said.

"Keeping it low key sounds like Doug. Okay, continue. Doug's in the hospital, your 16-year-old daughter is missing, and the police are looking for her. Is that right? And Doug told you to find me if anything happened to him, but he's getting better, right?"

"Yes, but there's more," Carol said. "After I got the call and went to the hospital, I didn't know what to do. I wanted to stay at the hospital with Doug, but I wanted to be home if Jane came home. I called my closest neighborhood friend, Mary, and had her meet me at the house. I told her Jane was missing and Doug was in the hospital. I begged her to keep it quiet and to bring a few things over and stay at our place so someone would be there in the event Jane came home. Bless her, she's such a rock. She was willing and said she would call me if anything at all happened around the house.

"It seemed like only a few hours later that Mary called to say that someone called the home phone asking for either Doug or me. When she told the caller we were not at home, they told her that they had left an important message in the mailbox at the front door and could she arrange to get it to us as soon as possible. She told him she would. She said she was feeling a little funny, not ha-ha funny but afraid funny, about opening the front door, but she put her fear aside, reached into the box, and came out with a McDonald's bag folded over a few times like a lumpy envelope. She was miffed that someone would be playing such pranks at such a serious time, but then again, nobody really knew what was going on but us.

"I had a fleeting thought that maybe it wasn't a poorly-planned hoax, that it was a premonition of sorts about the bag, but I didn't want to involve anyone else, and I didn't want to leave Doug's side. So I asked Mary to open it and see what was inside. I'll never forget it as long as I live. I heard her scream and then break down. Thank God she had gone inside. She kept saying my name over and over and asking me to come home.

"I left the hospital right away and when I got there, the bag contained not a single lock, but a big handful of Jane's hair and a note demanding money, $250,000, and that further contact would be made with drop off instructions. I sent Mary home after that."

"Okay," Sam said, "that gives us a possible reason for her disappearance anyway. Money! Some jerk wants money that's too damned lazy to work for it. It always comes down to money, but why her and why you or Doug?"

"We're clueless," Carol said.

"Back to the police. I'm surprised I haven't heard about it, or maybe I have but it didn't register. I imagine there must be a lot of good people working on it, and I know Doug's one heck of a capable man and probably directing the whole operation from his hospital bed. What have they come up with?"

"Not much at all," she whispered.

Sam frowned, thinking that this couldn't be happening again. How could two friends of his end up this way? He knew he would have to find Doug's daughter. Two weeks out was a long and dangerous time, and they needed him now more than anyone else he could think of.

"Where's Doug? What hospital?"

"He's at Kings County on Clarkson in Brooklyn."

Sam told Carol to stay put for a second, that they would go over together, but he had to make a phone call before they left.

He waited for a receptionist to put him through. "Hello, Dr. Meyers. This is Sam Rufus. I'm calling to let you know I have to cancel my next couple of appointments, and I wanted to tell you in person instead of leaving a message or not showing up.

"Not so fast, mister. We just got started. You're not ducking out on me so soon already, are you?" Brenda Meyers asked.

"No, not ducking out at all. Believe it or not, I think I'll enjoy talking to you. I'm sure it will ease my mind a little. My buddy, Doug Stone, needs my help in Brooklyn, so I have to go and check out a few things for him."

"Are you sure that's as important as getting yourself on track first?"

"Doug's daughter has disappeared and they need help finding her. He was shot and is in Kings County Hospital Center in Brooklyn. If you don't believe me, you can call the hospital if you want. I've got to go now, and I'll just have to face the consequences when I get back. I just wanted you to know I wasn't ducking out on you. I couldn't afford that on my resume."

"All right, Sam. I'll give you two weeks, and if you need more time, call me. I'll stall the judge if need be for as long as I can. Good luck, and I hope things work out for Doug Stone and his family. I'll be praying for them," Brenda Meyers said and hung up.

"All right, Carol, that's done," Sam called to her. "Hold on, let me pack a few things, and then we can go."

"Was that your wife on the phone?" Carol asked.

"No, my shrink. Nice lady, too."

He went into his closet, pulled a lever, and a drop-down compartment opened up. A big duffle bag tumbled out, and he started filling it up. He strapped on his double shoulder holster and slipped on a jacket. Next, two .357 Magnum revolvers with extended barrels, a pump-action shot gun, plastic explosives, ninja stars, knives, handcuffs, and enough ammo to take on an army just about filled his duffle. He slung it over his shoulder, tapped the shoulder holster, poured the Jack down the drain, and moved Carol out the door.

They took the elevator and walked out front to her parked car where the doorman stood smiling at Sam and his sister like a proud father. He handed her the keys.

"Carol, you've been through so much already, why don't you let me drive us to the hospital?" Sam asked.

Carol handed the keys to him, got in the passenger side, and started crying. Sam didn't pretend to know a lot about women and how they dealt with things like this, but he knew enough to see her nerves were frayed and that her emotions were close to exploding. She needed to release her tension, and what better place than the confines of her own car where she could cry and scream as loud and long as she wanted. He was glad she had found him and considered him part of her comfort zone.

"Sam, I didn't mean to spy on you, but since your door was open, I saw what you packed into your bag. Why would you need so much stuff?"

"I always pack heavy because I never know what I might be up against and what I'll need on the job."

"But why so many weapons at one time," Carol asked.

Sam drove around the corner to the lower garage, and stopped by his own vehicle. He opened its rear end, pulled back a screen, and took out a sniper rifle and tripod. "I almost forgot this, and the reason I need so much stuff and take so many weapons at one time is to be sure I have enough fire power without having to reload."

Chapter Ten

C arol was quiet by the time Sam started their drive over the newly re-decked Brooklyn Bridge. The bridge spanned just over a mile and traffic was at a near crawl. It was going to take a little longer to cross it today. Sam decided to try to get her thinking more positively, so he asked, "Exactly how long have you and Doug been married?"

"Two years next month," she replied.

"Congratulations. Hey, wait a minute. The last time I talked to Doug, he told me about this girl he had met. She had a daughter who was as cute as a button and ecstatic about turning thirteen. He seemed really happy and upbeat about the whole situation. That was about three years ago! Would you happen to be the girl he was referring to?"

"I hope so. It sounds like us. I didn't think Doug ever talked about us much to anyone. It's not his way, you know, and unless he knows someone really well, he keeps a pretty zipped lip. But I'll say this, he may be quiet on the outside, but he's got a lot inside him, and there's no better husband or father on the face of this earth than Douglas Jamison Stone."

"Well said, Carol. I couldn't agree more. He's a very lucky man! I can tell you really love him," Sam said.

"Thank you. I sure do!"

It took twenty minutes after they made it off the bridge to reach the hospital, but to both Carol and Sam it seemed like hours had passed by.

When they walked into Doug's room, it was empty, and the bed was newly made. Carol looked at Sam and lost it, immediately thinking the worst and turning to run. She nearly mowed down the doctor coming into the room and knocked the file from his hands. As he stooped to retrieve it and its contents, she lowered herself, too, and shrieked in his face. "Where's Doug? Where's my husband? What have you done with him?"

Sam took Carol by the elbow and helped her rise as the doctor replied, "Carol Stone? We've been trying to reach you for the past several hours. Your husband has definitely turned a good corner and is on the home stretch to being released. We'll want to watch him for 24 to 48 hours, and he's been transferred to a different room. He's been asking for you," the doctor said. "You will find him one floor up, Room 620, I think, but check at the station. If things continue as they have been, you'll have him back home in just a few more days. We'll see." Relief washed over Carol, and she and Sam thanked the doctor before racing to the new room.

As the door to 620 opened, Doug's eyes lit up, not only at the sight of his wife, but also for his old partner who followed behind her. After Carol kissed him, Doug said, "I see that you accomplished your mission. Good job, honey."

"I just followed your instructions. The rest was easy," Carol said.

Sam moved close to the bed now and shook Doug's hand. "Great to see you, but I'd rather it be under different circumstances. Why didn't you get in touch with me earlier?"

"You looked like you were too busy trying to keep from going to jail. We were following the details in the paper, and I told Carol if anything bad was to happen to me, she was to find you. Next thing you know, Jane disappeared, and I got shot. I don't recall how I ended up in the hospital, but the next thing I remember is waking up in here," Doug said.

"I'm here now, so catch me up on what you have so far, partner."

"It sounds good to hear you call me 'partner' again, Sam. I'll tell you that. Okay, here's the deal. A little after her sixteenth birthday, Jane got her driver's license to go along with that not-very-practical Mustang convertible we got her. She was going over to the Plaza to the movies with her friend

Jennifer. Jane told us it was a matinee that started around 4:30. We figured she would be home by 8:00 or 8:30 at the latest, but when she wasn't, we called Jennifer's house around nine thinking she might have lost track of time. Jen said she had dropped her off over an hour earlier. I drove toward Jennifer's house thinking maybe I would meet her somewhere along the way. There was no sign of her. We know she loves the water, so before I let myself go home or put out an all-points on her, I cruised through Marine Park trying to think like a teenager. You know, what kind of a cool route can I take back home with the heat on and the top down. Nothing at the park, so I thought I would hit Ramshead. Maybe she had gone to look at the boats, but it still didn't make sense. It was dark, and she knew not to hang out by the docks alone at night.

"It was a miracle that I spotted her car next to the construction site where they're rehabing those old warehouses into condos. The top was up, doors were closed, rear passenger tire was flat, and the spare was propped up against the car. She must have run over who knows what with all the trash and construction debris around the place. I drove by slowly scoping things out, then backed up to park directly in front of her car. My heart was leaping out of my chest. I grabbed a flashlight, and I have to tell you I was terrified of looking in the window and seeing her inside hurt or worse. But she wasn't there. Only her purse and her keys were sitting on the front seat.

"A fresh coating of dust from the lot and the day's construction had settled on the road where she had parked, and there were footprints around her car that looked like a scuffle had taken place. It looked like something or someone was being dragged across the road and onto the site through a section of chain link fencing that had been cut. The tracks stayed near the perimeter of the fence where things are pretty well concealed by overgrowth. I was casting my light back and forth, and then by a heap of old brick, I saw a sneaker, Jane's new Keds, red to match her car. I bent over and picked it up, and that's the last thing I remember except taking a hell of a blow in my back. Our dispatcher said I made a distress call, but for the life of me I don't remember doing it.

"And then, if that's not all, Carol confessed that she got a ransom demand the next morning after I came in here. I was so out of it for the first few days that she couldn't even tell me about it, so she called my family and hers, and they rounded up the money from God knows who all. That's another story. She missed the first drop off date. She went, but nobody showed up. They must have been feeling some heat. The next day, they called the house and left a message on the recorder with Jane's voice telling us that Saturday is the next big day and somebody would be back in touch. We're waiting right now to know exactly where and when to make the drop. We've got the whole force ready, but we're still clueless where Jane is."

"Have they checked out where you found her car and shoe and all? That seems like a no-brainer," Sam said.

The short answer was that the area had been checked and there was no sign of Jane. Doug answered a non-stop flurry of questions that Sam had for him and gave him all the facts he could remember that might be useful. Carol added information about her daughter, and Sam wrote down what he thought he would need to refer to in the next few hours or days.

"Motive seems to be money. Carol and I had already talked about that. Could be random, or you could have enemies. Got any ideas?" Sam asked.

"You know how it is in this business, Sam. We always have enemies, but not Carol and Jane."

"Doesn't seem fair sometimes, does it?"

"Goes with the territory. It's one of the first things we learn. I've been laying here racking what's left of my drugged-out brain. A while back, I was working on a drug case. The dealer shot two people point blank, both of them in the face. It's a long and sickening story, but he made some messy mistakes that led us to him. We had been watching him for a while. Then we got him, locked him up, and he's been waiting for his fry day. Grady Wallace."

"Wallace?" Sam asked.

"Yes, Grady Wallace. Why do you ask?"

"Do you know if he has a brother named Sidney? He's doing time for serious assault and battery, and that may not be all."

"It could be, I don't recall. Grady Wallace has been locked up for a pretty long time now. The jury gave him what he deserved, if you know what I mean. Here's the kicker. About a year ago, I got a letter at the precinct. Some Neanderthal scribbling in an unmarked envelope that said if Grady Wallace died, someone very close to me would die, too. That's all it said. It scared the hell out of me. I took the note seriously, looking up the facts about Grady Wallace that had gotten blurry with time. It worried me for a while, but there's always some kind of weirdness going on. I turned the note over at the department to see if it could be tracked down, but nothing ever came of it, I never heard another word, and I chocked it up to there being too many nuts out there running around loose."

"When is Grady Wallace going for his injection?" Sam asked.

"The 28th," Doug said.

Sam released an involuntary groan. "Doug, it's the 27th," he said.

"I know. I've been so drugged up I hardly knew my own name, and like I said, I put this thing aside long ago. You don't think there's anything to this, do you?

Sam just looked at him and said nothing.

"I have to get out of here!" Doug said.

"Doug, you're not going anywhere right now. You need to concentrate on getting your broken body fixed, and it sounded from the doctor that you might be good to go in a few days. Please. You've managed to get me over here, you've told me the problem, given me a good head start, and now it's best if you let me solve things. Don't get in my way, and don't do anything that will hold me back from finding Jane. You'll only slow me down. Give me your mobile phone numbers, and I'll keep in touch with you. Besides, Carol needs you right here by her side for now," Sam said.

"Okay, partner. I agree that you'll have to go this one alone. I've got every confidence in you, Sam. I know if she can be found, you'll be the one to find her," Doug said.

"Thanks. Whoever these creeps are, I think it's time for them to meet the Hurricane. Do either of you have a recent picture of Jane? I'd hate to mess up and take out the wrong people. One other thing, I've got my gear already loaded in Carol's car. It would save us some critical minutes if I could take it and get down to business."

Carol handed her keys back to Sam. "Take it. I don't care about the car. Please just bring our daughter back home alive." Carol dug in her purse for a photo. "Here she is, almost three weeks ago on her birthday."

Sam said goodbye and walked down the hall. He had a very short time to cover a very large city. He would check out the area Doug talked about first. He was just hoping Jane was still alive and unharmed because if they had harmed her, may God save them because this Hurricane would not.

Chapter Eleven

Sam drove directly to Ramshead Bay, the last place Doug remembered before the lights went out. He parked Carol's car in the spot he believed was precisely where Jane's car had been parked. Outside, he scanned the immediate area carefully.

Dust, a few flurries, and the noisy work of construction filled the air, and workmen scurried about like ants across the street. A crane with a wrecker ball swung slowly into position at a warehouse building and then stopped as its operator climbed down. Sam watched things from the road for an hour or so and noted that a hole in the chain link fence had been repaired with bits of twisted wire. When he had memorized the site, he left. He would come back later.

Looking at his watch, it was 9:00 p.m. when Sam arrived back at the construction site. A full moon illuminated the sky and the grounds. Had it not been for the heavy brush and high weeds at the fence line, he would not have needed his flashlight, but he was looking for anything that would help this case. He clipped the wire-patched fence and began his approach along the perimeter to the warehouse buildings. He noted the old brick pile Doug had talked about and the toppled bricks that may have snagged Jane's shoe. It wasn't far from here, according to Doug, that he had been struck from behind.

All seemed quiet. There were no signs of guard dogs, which he had prepared for, or night watchmen. He made his way slowly in the direction of the crane with its wrecking ball eerily poised and ready to strike.

Sam's stomach started talking to him. He had been shining his light from side to side for signs of disrupted soil, not the bulldozed soil that now dominated the site, but that which might indicate something had been recently dug and buried. He checked his thoughts. Too macabre. He was heading away from the perimeter fence crossing the scraped surface of the land with its piles of debris and discarded drink bottles, when a shell casing from a .45 presented itself, the same kind that had wounded Doug. Sam picked up the casing with his knife and slipped it into a bag.

He neared the entrance of the first abandoned building. Its painted Brooklyn Wharf & Warehouse letters were barely still legible. His stomach was rumbling now, and it was as accurate as a barometer. He had a feeling he was so close he could almost touch her. As he walked inside, he looked behind him and saw a flickering light on the second floor of the old building next door. Then, as if on queue, he saw a figure in the window. It was too far away to see much more than the form itself. *Why didn't I see that when I first arrived,* Sam asked himself. Both buildings looked dark and vacant. Most of their windows were broken out, doors were hanging or missing, and the aged, mossy bricks were pried loose by vines and wind.

Sam stepped inside the warehouse before him. He saw no movement and heard no sounds within. When he was certain all was clear around him, he switched off his flashlight and did a quick sprint toward the building with the flickering light. The side door with rusty hinges was open. Sam slowly entered, noting the steel staircase that connected the two floors. It must have been one of the old tobacco inspection buildings. Its conveyor rails were scattered about, and the smell of the plant had permeated the wooden beams.

Sam was hypersensitive to the passing time. If ever there was a case of time being of the essence, it was now. He was standing still and getting his bearings when he heard laughter coming from the floor above. He could hear at least two different voices. Slowly, he crept up the open stairs to the second floor. Unlike the largely open first floor, the second floor was divided into rooms. A dim light came out from the bottom of the fourth door down the hall. Sam positioned himself across from it, his back against the wall. He drew his gun from his shoulder holster and slowly cocked the hammer back. To prevent the old door from splintering when he kicked it in, he aimed directly for its hardware.

The door flew open with a loud crack to reveal two men sitting on the floor with a small fire burning between them and bedrolls unfurled and waiting.

"I'm sorry, sir. We'll leave right away. We didn't know anyone else was here," one man said.

"No, that's quite all right. It is I who should apologize to you. I was looking for someone, a young lady, and I thought she might be here. My name is Sam," he said, walking over to them and extending his hand.

"That there is Fred, and I'm Harry," the first man replied as he shook Sam's hand. "Maybe we know what you're looking for. I don't know for sure, but some men went into that there building over yonder maybe about a week or so ago. Didn't see them right away after that, but then, after a few days, every night and morning when the worker men ain't around, one of them comes, stays maybe half an hour, and then goes. He's usually carrying something when he comes in, like a grocery bag maybe. Don't know what it is that's being carried or what they're doing, and besides, we don't want no trouble ourselves."

"Did they have a girl with them when you first saw them all together?" Sam asked.

"Can't really be sure, but the time four went in and only three came out, one of them had long hair and was smaller. We never thought about going over and checking it out. We ain't as young as we used to be. Our eyesight's not so keen either, and even if it was, like I said, we can't afford to go looking for no trouble," Fred said.

"We usually don't hear nothing, but the other night we heard a guy hollering over there by the fence. He was saying something about stopping whining and getting to it, and something about somebody's daddy better get busy," Harry said.

"Then a few days ago, a gun shot woke us up. It sounded like it came from over there. When we heard that gunfire, we hid low and closed our eyes. We stayed that way until we felt the sun shining on us in the morning and saw the coast was clear, but we never saw signs of nobody being dead. We still see them going into that building. Don't know why or what they're up to and don't care as long as they don't come over here."

"When was the last time you saw them," Sam asked.

"I think it was last night. There were three of 'em. I don't remember seeing the one man this morning though," Fred said. "Let's see, yes, it was yesterday they were here twice; the first time was early morning when it's first getting light and then again a little before the sun goes down. The one comes about every morning and late evening, so he should be showing up any time. He don't stay too long, maybe fifteen minutes to a half hour, and then he gets in his car and rumbles off," Harry said. "Nobody's ever come over here. We're pretty quiet, but sometimes when it gets cold like this, we have to make a little fire, and we get scared about somebody running us off, or worse."

"Aren't you curious about what they're doing over there?" Sam asked.

"Take a good look at us son. Even if we stuck our nose into their business or had a mind to blow the whistle on them, who would believe a couple bums like us?" Fred said.

Sam took out two twenty dollar bills and said, "Don't sell yourselves short, fellas. I appreciate what you've told me. Here's a little extra spending money and my phone number. I'm going to head over and take a look around myself, but if you ever need help or hear or see signs of a young lady over there or around here, call me right away, will you? And if you don't have any money, just tell the operator to dial me direct, and I'll pay for your call."

"We really appreciate your help, son, but who are you again, and who did you say we should ask for?" Harry asked.

"Just tell them you're looking for Hurricane, and they'll patch you through," Sam said.

"Hurricane? I've heard that name. Are you that guy in the newspaper we saw?" Harry asked.

"Yes, that's probably me, Harry. When this is over, I promise to look you up and say hello. Right now, I need to find out if the person I'm looking for is inside that building, and you guys need to look for a new place to bunk down. Your home sweet home here is about to become a pile of rubble, and I've got a bad feeling about company coming tonight."

Chapter Twelve

Sam's adrenalin was pumping as he sprinted the distance between the two buildings. When he arrived at the side of the building he now thought Jane was in, he pressed himself into its blackened brick shadows and went all the way around it so he understood its exits and entrances. He returned to the rear of the building that faced the waterfront. The old wooden roll-up dock door was raised a good two feet off the floor. Sam lifted it a bit more and made his way inside.

It didn't take long to discover the young woman's body stretched out on its side and illumined by moonlight among the discarded crates and empty beer bottles. She lay directly on the concrete floor, her long curly hair swirled in a pool at the back of her neck, and below her jeans a foot missed its shoe. She had to be cold.

Feeling fairly confident that he was alone except for the girl, Sam quickly returned to the dock doors, knocked on them and called out to make his presence known. All he heard in return was his stomach telling him to get back to Jane, and quickly.

Sam kneeled by her. Her eyes were closed, and she was not moving. He put his hand on her shoulder and shook her gently. "Jane, is that you?" he asked. Her head came up lethargically, and he saw she was bound at the neck by a dog's choke chain that was attached by cable to a piece of machinery.

"Don't be afraid, Jane. My name is Sam, and I'm here to take you home. Your mother and father sent me to find you." Sam took out his flashlight and the picture Carol gave him and, after viewing it himself, turned it around for her to look at.

Sam noticed her hands were cuffed together and bound to the machinery as well. She clutched a gold locket around her neck. He had noticed it in the photograph Carol had given him, and before he left the hospital, she had told him how this single piece of jewelry meant the world to her daughter. Doug had the wheels in motion to adopt Jane as soon and he and Carol married. Years prior, Jane's own father had become more and more absent. He was a drummer in a rock band that had started having local touring success, and he liked the rail-thin groupies and applause more than going home to a wife with milky hips and a child that demanded things of him he got no joy in giving. Homebound fatherhood was not his gig. He had all but disappeared from their life when she filed for divorce. There would be no child support. When Doug's own mother passed away and her possessions were put in order, the old locket his father had given her surfaced. One photo nestled itself inside the heart, a photo of the three of them—father, mother, son, a loving and enduring family. Doug would do the same for Jane, and it was their photo now—Doug, Carol, and Jane, her family—that she held onto. She shuttered, fully awake now and frightened. Her legs kicked out at him as she sat up and tested her bondage. "Who are you, mister?"

"My name is Sam, Jane, but if you like, you can call me 'Hurricane'. I am here to take you home. Your parents are worried about you."

"What time is it?" Jane asked.

"It's about nine-thirty or ten o'clock. Why do you ask?"

"I should be getting a visitor soon. He comes twice every day with food for me, and he's late," she said.

"Is it just one man that comes?"

"Yes, mostly, except for the first few times. They brought me here once, then took me away, then brought me back again. I haven't seen all of them together since."

"Jane, are you strong enough to help me set a trap for your visitor? Sam asked.

"Yes, I think so. What do you want me to do?" Jane asked.

Sam undid her cuffs and then the choke chain around her neck. Jane sat up and rubbed her wrists and neck, moving her head in a circular direction to work out the stiffness.

"I'm filthy, and I stink," she said near tears. "I can hardly remember the last time I had a bath or brushed my teeth."

"Don't worry about that on my account. You might be filthy for now, but you're free and will be back to all the comforts of home soon, I promise. Right now, though, we're going to lay you back down and make these things look like they're still in tact. When he comes inside, you'll look and act like you're still tied up. I'll do the rest," Sam said.

"Okay, I can do that, and I think it's about time they get a taste of their own medicine," she said.

"Dispensing a healthy dose of good medicine to bad people is what I do best. When your jailer shows up to feed you, I hope to be able to thank you for your assistance and call someone to take you home. But, if things start getting rough and complicated, if we get some bad surprises, we'll have to get you out of sight and out of harm's way, pronto! Do we have a deal?" Sam asked.

She gave him a small smile, finally understanding and trusting that he was there to help her. Sam let her know that when the time came, she should not look his way until he made his move, no matter what happened.

A car's engine and tires crunching on gravel was audible, and it surprised Sam as he hadn't factored in car access to the site. The sound the car made when it was turned off prompted Jane to tell Sam that it was him; she recognized the wheeze it made before going silent. She was suddenly jumpy with worry.

"Settle down, Jane, and remember our plan. I'm here to help you, and everything's going to be okay," Sam said helping her to lie back down and move into position.

He stood behind a stack of wooden crates and heard footsteps coming in their direction. It was a heavy step made by a big person, Sam thought, and coming from the front of the building in no particular hurry.

Jane was lying down in her usual position bound by cables to the menacing machine that dominated the room. The man came into view—a tall, gawky silhouette with a head of wild hair that triggered visions of Albert Einstein and Charles Manson. He carried nothing in his hand, not the food that Jane had expected. He approached her, kicked her lightly against her shoeless foot. She stirred slightly, playing her part well.

"Sorry to say, doll face," he said standing over her, "but tomorrow's a special pickup and drop off day, and we're seriously running out of time and patience. We're going to have a little change of plans. It seems like your irresponsible father hasn't come up with anything for us to pick up. He must not care as much about you as you thought, so I'm afraid it's time to say goodbye." He pulled a plastic bag from the pocket of his jeans and stood a step closer to her.

"Now, that was a terrible thing for you to say," Hurricane said.

"What the …!" he said as he turned to the voice and a saw a .357 Magnum staring back at him.

"As you should have known, her father hasn't catered to your every special delivery request because he's still in the hospital where you put him when you shot him two weeks ago, slobbo. Furthermore, you had no intensions of letting the girl go. You would have killed her no matter what. Isn't that the way you creeps operate?" Sam hissed.

"Who the hell are you?"

"I'm your worst nightmare in living color," Sam said, shining a flashlight in the man's face, "and I want some answers about you and your buddies."

The man made a quick assessment of Sam. He had several inches on him and a few years, but Hurricane's angles were sharp and chiseled, and his build looked strong and solid as opposed to his own slender frame. He thought for a moment to bring his hands up and dislodge the gun, but he was certain the odds weren't stacked in his favor.

"I'm working alone," he snapped.

"You have no idea how glad I am to hear you say that because after what I'm going to put you through, you'll beg me to kill you. I already know that you have at least two others working with you, so this will give me a chance to vent some frustration that's been building up in me lately," Sam said.

"How do you know about two other guys? Nobody's seen anything. You're just fishing. I think I smell a cop searching for answers. I was paid to come down here, feed this girl, and take her out to piddle. That's all I know."

"Who is it that pays you?" Hurricane asked.

"Wouldn't you like to know? You'll have to ask me nicer than that if you want information out of me."

Sam cocked his gun, grinned, and then came up under the guy's chin so hard with the flashlight that he snapped back against the concrete floor and laid still. Sam emptied his hands, delicately removed Jane's cuffs and chains, and helped her to her feet.

"You knocked him out with one punch," Jane said smiling. "But what is going on with my father? They shot him? He's in the hospital? Is he going to be okay?"

"I'm sorry you had to hear about your father this way, but he started searching for you the minute he called your friend the day of the movie and she said you had dropped her off. He wanted to find you himself before calling in help. When he found your car and saw signs of a scuffle by it and tracks leading toward the building, he was coming for you. They shot him and left him to die, but your father is too tough of a man. He was able to call for help, and somebody got him out of there and to the hospital. After he came to, and this was after your mother had somehow found me and brought me to the hospital, that's when he told me where he had seen your car, and that is how I found you so fast," Sam said.

"So my father does care about me after all?" Jane said.

"Absolutely! There was never a question about that. That jerk was just talking out his ... never mind. There's no question about it," Sam said, "and I think there's nothing more he needs right now than to know you are safe and on your way home. Let's get you out of here. I'll call your parents, and your dad can send an officer to pick you up. From here on, I've got a hunch things might get more hectic, and there's not going to be enough time or enough left of me to babysit tonight," Sam said.

"No! I want to stay. I can help you. I'll know if he's lying about his buddies. Remember, I saw them, all three of them, herding me out here in the first place after I dropped Jennifer off. It was easy for them to run me off the street like a dog. I might be a new driver, but it took them a while. My car started driving funny, and when they finally forced me over, all three of them got out, and I saw them all. And they are the last thing I saw until all this. I'll recognize them if they come back," Jane said.

Sam watched her and rubbed his chin. He wasn't sure what or who to expect next, but he knew they should stay put for a while and see. "It's against my better judgment, but all right, you can stay. However, you need to be out of sight, and if you get the least bit squeamish on me, it's off to your parents you go," Hurricane said.

"After what they put me through, him especially, I deserve to see what they get," Jane said.

"You are definitely Doug Stone's daughter, no doubt about that!"

Chapter Thirteen

S am looked the room over in the dim moonlight. Heavy machinery dominated the center, its use unidentifiable in the darkness. There were wooden crates and what looked like dilapidated library tables and chairs below a large section of missing ceiling that exposed heavy wooden rafters. He chose a chair, picked up Jane's abductor by the back of his pants, and securely tied him to it. Locating the section of cable that had bound Jane to the machinery, he threw it over a rafter and hoisted the chair with its new occupant into the air.

When the man awoke, he soon realized he was tied up in a chair in a dark building and suspended about three feet off the floor from a ceiling rafter. "What the hell is going on here? Where am I? How did I get here?"

"First of all, watch you're language, we have a little lady present. Second, you're in no position to demand anything, and last but not least, since you're awake now, let's have a little talk, starting with you telling me your name," Hurricane said.

When his eyes finally focused, he saw Hurricane standing in front of him holding a two by four about three-foot long. Then he realized his ankles had been bound to the chair with duct tape in such a way that they were tucked under him, making his knees vulnerable and tilting his body precariously forward. He was exactly eye level with Hurricane. When he didn't respond with his name, Hurricane raised the two by four and swung it full strength hitting the man's left kneecap. There was a swish, a crack, and a bloody scream as the pain raced through his body.

"Now that I have your undivided attention, unless you want to end up three feet shorter than you are now, how would you like to cooperate and answer some very simple questions?"

Again, there was no response, only what looked like an icy, defiant stare. Hurricane raised the two by four and brought it against the other knee. When Jane heard his agonizing scream, she felt sorry for him, but only for an instant.

She walked over to him and spat in his face. "Here's my thanks to you, you piece of filth, you who gave me no privacy and nothing to clean myself with, you who sat here with your pants unzipped and ran your dirty fingers over me, you with your nasty beer breath. You wouldn't know a toothbrush if one bit you. You're despicable, and you should be ashamed of yourself," she said starting to cry. Instead of crumbling, however, she braced herself, spat again, and stepped back as Sam came forward.

"You sound like a pretty rotten guy, a rotten guy with probably a rotten name, so what is it? Once again, and for the last time, tell me who you are," Sam said as he raised the board.

Even in low light, the man saw a raging inferno in Hurricane's eyes, and just before Hurricane drew the two by four back for its final blow, he yelled, "Toby, Toby Sanders! My name is Toby Sanders."

"Well, Toby, Toby Sanders, that wasn't so difficult, was it? My name is Hurricane, and now that we're on a first name basis, who are you and your friends working for?"

"What friends?" Toby said. "I don't know what you're talking about."

Without a warning, Sam came up with the board like an underhand pitch and struck it just below his left knee. This time, all that was heard was the sound of splintering bone. Toby Sanders' head flew backward and swirled with the impact. He opened his mouth to release his pain, but screaming was beyond him. His head fell forward as the chair swung in the air.

"Don't pass out on me yet. I'm just getting started. If you don't start answering my questions, you will never be able to walk on your two feet again. And don't worry, if you pass out, I will keep reviving you until you tell me what I want to hear. If that takes unreasonably long, you might as well start considering what it's going to be like to be a vegetable for the rest of your miserable life. Now, start talking, or suffer the consequences," Hurricane said.

"You're that cop who was on trial that they showed on television," Toby cried out.

"Toby, if you saw that, then you also know that I was suspended for thirty days. Therefore, legally, I'm not a cop at this time."

"You're no better than I am, man. I'll testify against you in court for excessive force all over again, and they'll put you away before they do me!"

"First of all, punk, I am better than you. For starters, I have two good legs." Hurricane swung the board once again, this time striking the man's knee with the two-inch side of the board. He swung it with such force that after the crack echoed in the room, the leg bone disengaged from the knee and was held in place only by the blood-stained pants that contained it and the tape securing his ankles to the chair. Toby wailed and turned white as the blood drained from his face.

"Now, if you would like to have at least one good leg left to stand on, you better stop screwing around, and start answering my questions. If you don't know who hired you and your friends, let's start all over again with you telling me who your friends are." When there was only whimpering and no answer, Sam raised the board again as if to strike.

"Okay! Okay! I'll talk. Just don't hit me again," Toby pleaded.

Sam lowered the board. "So help me, if you lie to me, I'll bust you up so badly nobody will recognize you. Now talk!"

Toby opened up and spilled over like a waterfall. "Steve Swenson. He's about six-foot-two, three hundred pounds, and just released from prison."

"What was he in prison for?" Sam asked.

"Rape. He raped some college girl and did two years. The other guy, Chris Cobalt, he's the crazy one. Him and his brother, Jim, were pushing cannabis, dust, and all kinds of whack when I met them. They got hooked up with a local guy who was in with a ring out of Mexico and were doing pretty good for a while. The big guy went down hard a while back and is still boxed for blowing away a couple of small-time runners that didn't pay up. Jimmy and Chris tried to do it on their own, but they both got busted. I heard two teenaged kids might have died from the crap they were selling, laced with too much shit. The brothers were tried, and both got off because the cops were caught fiddling with the evidence. They got themselves a shrewd attorney and walked out free men. As far as I know, Chris was the one with the idea about kidnapping the girl, and he'll be the one that will hand-to-hand me and Steve in a few more days. There may have been somebody above him, but I don't know who. I think Chris is the one who shot that cop when he caught him snooping around over here. I don't think he knew it was the girl's old man," Toby said.

"Not only is he the girl's father, he's my partner. Now, where can I find these outstanding friends of yours?"

"I'm afraid that if I tell you where they are, they'll kill me."

"Believe me, Toby, when I meet these guys, you won't have to worry about them. But, on the other hand, if you don't tell me, what do you think I will do to you?"

"It wasn't my idea to kidnap the girl. I was just doing my job and having a little harmless fun with her. I didn't hurt her, and if you promise that they won't kill me, I'll tell you," Toby said.

"I think eventually you'll tell me anyway, but I promise you that if they try to resist me, you won't have to look over your shoulder anymore."

"Okay then. There's Steve Swenson, the big one. He's working as a cook not very far from here. I don't know the name of the place. He's always bragging about their world-class burgers. Chris Cobalt, now he's a genuine scumbag. He's still dealing and making himself out to be a big player, dressing flashy, showing off, but he's working down on the shipping docks, too. It makes a good cover. It's a warehouse for food supplies somewhere over there by the bone yard. Both of them are supposed to meet me here tonight around eleven. We had to make some decisions about the girl and what to do with her body."

"I'll bet you did," Sam said looking at his watch. It read ten-thirty. *Chris Cobalt.* The name sounded familiar. Jim Cobalt, too, but why and from where? He would have to think about that later. His pulse quickened, and he felt the hair stand up on the back of his neck. He had a plan.

As he lowered Toby to the floor, he warned him, "Your information better be right, or I personally will make your life an extremely painful one." He picked up Toby by the back of the chair he was tied to and motioned for Jane to open the door.

"Stay close, Jane, and alongside us," he said. At first, she had thought Hurricane was much meaner than her abductors, but he knew how to get the answers he was looking for. That was for sure.

They crossed the distance to the other building. Sam figured it was a better vantage point for his sniper rifle, and it would keep the girl farther away from harm.

Sam placed the chair with Toby still securely bound to it under the tallest part of the open metal stairway. He secured the cable to the second stair from the top and fastened it so that Toby was lifted off the floor by a foot or so and left swinging without the benefit of being too close to a wall. He had learned that suspending one in this way reduced the risk of them using anything—floors, walls, doors, or window frames—to turn the chair and free themselves.

Sam turned to Jane. "It's time to call your folks." He pulled out his cell and dialed a number. "Carol, this is Sam," he said quickly. "How's Doug doing? I need you to have him send an officer over to Ramshead Bay right away to pick Jane up. She's alive and well, and she would like to come home. Have them meet us at the front gate of the Viridian Condominiums construction site. That's on the Shore Boulevard side."

"Doug's fine, he's going to make the call right now to get someone there. What about you? Your job is done. Can't you both just get in my car and come here?" Carol said to Sam.

"No, Carol, my job has just begun. I have a little unfinished business that needs to be addressed."

Sam and Jane left the building. They stayed close to the perimeter fence, on alert for traffic of any kind, and waited at the entrance for her ride. When the squad car was out of sight, Sam went to Carol's car and retrieved the big duffle bag he had packed in Manhattan.

Upon returning to the building, he found Toby spinning in the chair trying to swing it against the wall.

"Toby, Toby, Toby. I thought you were smarter than that. You're secured in such a way that if you break that chair while you're suspended, your arms will snap backward and most likely be torn from your body. That was a little technique I learned from a Chinese-American soldier when I was in Guam," Sam said.

It was time for Sam to get ready for some company. Eleven o'clock was right around the corner. He purposefully opened up his duffle bag where Toby could see it and understand the harsh justice that would soon rain down on his accomplices. Hurricane emptied it piece by piece. Toby became fully alert and very still, his eyes the size of saucers. He couldn't believe the weapons that were crammed inside, not just the sheer number of them, but the nature of things he had never seen before.

Chapter Fourteen

When Sam had finished emptying his duffle bag, it yielded all the weaponry he had stuffed into it from his closet in Manhattan—two .357 Magnum revolvers with extended barrels, a pump-action shotgun, plastic explosives, ninja stars, knives, handcuffs, and plenty of ammunition, as well as an M-16 automatic rifle, and two .45 automatic hand guns. With that and the two pieces he packed in his shoulder holster, he had enough fire power to kill an army, but the most impressive weapon was yet to be seen. He pulled out his sniper rifle with its own tripod.

When he started setting up the tripod, Toby said, "You can't be serious! Do you really think you can hit anybody from this distance? That building must be at least a hundred yards away."

"It's more like one fifty, give or take a yard or two," Hurricane said.

"Are you nuts?" Toby asked.

"We'll soon find out, won't we? Furthermore, if you interrupt me again or make as much as another peep, I'm going to stick a gag in your mouth. Do you understand? Matter of fact, we'll just get that out of the way now, in case you're tempted to tip off your pals."

Sam took a gag from his duffle bag and tied it in place over Toby's mouth just as he spotted headlights. Either Toby had left the gate ajar or they were in cahoots with somebody with a key and were driving through the site like it belonged to them. They drove in a straight line to the building that had housed Jane.

"It looks like your eleven o'clock date has arrived to make some decisions about the girl's body, the same body that's on its way home, safe and sound, where she belongs." He grabbed his binoculars for a closer look.

The car came to a stop in front of the building they had vacated less than thirty minutes earlier. The headlights were switched off, and two guys stepped out. The driver stood six-something and looked like he weighed in around three-hundred pounds. This had to be Steve Swenson, the cook Toby had spoken of. Probably just off work and smelling like burgers. About the same time, Hurricane saw the passenger, shorter than himself even, come around the front of the car. He looked like he was dressed for the opera. Sam's powerful binoculars, aided by the moonlight and patchy high pressure sodium perimeter lights, panned him from his slicked-back hair to the expensive shoes he wore. He figured that Swenson must be there in the capacity of bodyguard to Chris Cobalt.

Right after the squad car had taken Jane away, Sam had dipped into his duffle bag for a couple of battery-operated microphones. One he rigged at the entrance of the building Jane had been in, and the second, he placed outside near Toby's car and what he considered the logical approach to the building. Before he had gone back inside to Toby to unload and assemble his arsenal, he had put on a wireless headset and tested it. And now there was sound.

"Where's Toby? Didn't I tell him to meet us here out front?" the shorter one, assumed to be Chris Cobalt, said.

"Maybe he's just late. Give him a few more minutes. He will be out," Swenson replied.

"I can't wait, and you can't either. We've got more stops to make in the next twelve hours, and they're a lot more important than this one. Maybe he's inside having a little too much fun. Let's get in there, do this job, and get out of here," Chris Cobalt said.

They went in together and saw only the empty handcuffs still bound to the machinery.

"What the hell is going on? Where's the girl? Where's Toby? So help me, if he screws this up, he's a dead man."

"Relax, Chris. Maybe he's got her out back for a final bathroom break. But I was sure he would keep her bound. He knows that much. Or maybe he's a step ahead of us and out in back burying the body," Steve said.

Sam heard them moving around, overturning crates, cursing, checking out the room Jane had been held in. After hearing a few things being broken inside the building, Sam heard, "For his sake, Steve, I hope you're right. But may the Lord help him if he messes this one up."

"Toby's been with us a long time. He wouldn't be stupid enough to double cross us, or the boss," Steve said.

"You're probably right. Let's check out the rest of the building for any signs of foul play. You take the upstairs. I'll finish looking around down here and check out back. They can't be far. His car's right here," Chris said. "Let's meet out front in five or ten minutes and talk about Plan B."

Sam heard the conversation and readied himself for the clean shot he would take, a shot intended to surprise them and only wound them so he could get information he needed to get to the bottom of things. He would steady his nerves and wait for the perfect shot. Within a few minutes, the opportunity came knocking, as Chris and Steve walked away from the building and back toward the car.

Sam crouched in the side door facing the two men and was slowly squeezing the trigger. Just before the shot got off, he heard what sounded like a squeal from in back of him. Toby had tried to yell, but he was muzzled, and the only sound the men heard was Sam's sniper rifle.

Steve pushed Chris to the ground and took the impact of the first shot, which nearly took his left arm clean off his body. That first shot had been intended for Chris. Sam was upset with himself as he took aim again at Chris until he saw Steve looking back at him with his own rifle. Sam and Steve squeezed off a shot simultaneously toward each other. Sam's bullet went through Steve's sight glass, hitting him in the eye. Steve's bullet nearly grazed Hurricane's left arm, and because of its angle and velocity, hit Toby in the chest as he swung in the chair.

Chris had half-crawled, half run toward the building. After shooting out the car's tires, Sam stood up and tapped his holstered .357 Magnum, grabbed his two .45s and an extra bullet clip. He walked toward Steve and the car knowing it would be harder now to find Chris. When he finally made it to the shooting area, Steve was lying in the dirt at the front of the car with the back of his head gone.

Sam was disappointed in his shot. He was hoping to take him alive. For certain now, he would need to salvage Chris. Sam found a slight but definite trail of blood heading toward what looked like a water tower in the corner of the property. Chris must have caught a piece of the bullet after all. The trail suddenly ended. Sam followed the prints and blood from half-way to the tower back to the rear of the building. Chris must have changed his mind about where he was going. One thing he could be sure of, the get-away car wouldn't be going anywhere fast with flat tires. At the rear of the building where Sam had first entered at the dock door, a ladder attached itself to the wall and gave access to the roof. Drops of blood splattered the crumbling slab beneath it. When Sam looked up the ladder to the roof, he saw Chris holding a gun pointed directly at him.

"Drop it or die," Hurricane called and took aim.

The sudden action and command surprised Chris. He acted like he was dropping the weapon and then suddenly turned it back in his hands and fired a shot. Hurricane had been faster, and his bullet hit Chris in the stomach, loosening his hold on his gun as it plunged to the ground near Sam's feet. Chris doubled over from his stomach wound and looked in danger of falling off the roof. Sam told him to stay where he was and approached the ladder to climb it. When Sam reached the rooftop, Chris had fallen over and was holding himself.

"Chris Cobalt, I need to know who you are working for, and I need to know now."

"I never wanted to hurt the girl, honest," Chris said, struggling for breath.

"Listen, before you die, tell me who hired you to shoot my partner and kidnap his daughter."

"Who the hell are you, anyway?" Chris asked.

"My name is Hurricane. I want you to tell me who hired you, Cobalt." There had been two people who weren't family with the same last name on the list from the Bureau of Prisons, brothers. It clicked with him now.

Chris's blood pumped from his wound and was blotted by his expensive shirt and suit. His hands were still clutching and working to keep himself together, but he was weakening, and his body was starting to twitch involuntarily. He slumped all the way over and was on his knees with his face in the gravel of the old ballasted roof. Sam came in close to his face.

"Tell me, Cobalt. Tell me who it is you go to. Give yourself a chance to buy a little redemption before it's too late. Is it Sidney Wallace?"

Cobalt sputtered, "It was C, C ..." was all he said before his body gave up and slumped to its side.

Hurricane shook him, but the body was limp. He checked the pulse. There was none. Taking him by the wrists, Hurricane lowered himself and Cobalt's body down the ladder. Once on the ground, he carried him around to the front of the building and laid him next to Steve. He went through the finely stitched Armani pockets. In the pants, nothing. In the inside jacket pocket, a comb, tube of lip balm, sizable clip of cash, and a piece of paper folded over many times. Sam carefully peeled the paper open. It was a list, a list of names he had seen before, and not so long ago.

Chapter Fifteen

Sam left them, bloodied and mangled, lying on the ground by their car—one big cook smelling like a hamburger and now looking like one, and the other one on the wrong end of dressed to kill. He was relieved for Jane's sake to have gotten her away in time to be spared the gruesomeness of it. It was an image that would possibly never fade, as if she hadn't seen enough already. He would call shortly in accordance with police protocol to arrange for bodies, vehicles, and details of the scene, but for now, he retrieved his speakers and walked back into the building where Toby was still hanging.

Deep, wretched despair and outrageous excitement coursed simultaneously through him. He had not gotten what he wanted—the open and flowing information about who the men were, what they were ultimately up to, if Sidney Wallace was behind them, and then what. Chris's attempt at a final utterance yielded nothing, but the note—a copy of the same note found on the gunman in Staten Island — propelled him forward.

He dropped the microphones into his duffle and looked at the scene beneath the steps. Toby's stifled cry had distracted his aim, but what if it had been unchecked and somehow reached Chris and Steve. It could be him there, his life bleeding out of him, him having gasped his last breath.

"Why did you have to yell?" he asked the corpse. "I might have been able to take Steve and Chris back alive, if not for that stupid stunt."

Sam gathered his weapons and packed his duffle bag. He walked up the stairs, stepping over the cable that suspended Toby's chair, and looked at him from above, another life wasted and gone.

Fred and Harry had pulled their sleeping bags into a corner and sat there huddled, not knowing if the next shots they heard would be meant for them. Sam spoke to them slowly and quietly, thanking them for staying out of the way. He had found the girl he was looking for. She had been kidnapped by some bad men who were holding her in the building across the way until her family paid them money. There had been shootings and death, and he was sorry they had been so close to it. The police would be there soon. There would be a lot of them, and they would be everywhere in the buildings, so if they knew of anywhere else to go, now might be the time.

He left the two of them and came back down, gathering his bag and leaving in his wake three dead men whose words and cooperation might have prevented every bit of this.

Carol's car embraced him. It was a silent shelter that put a protective shield of glass and metal between him and the carnage. He placed the bag in the rear seat, switched on the dash lights, and took the note out of his pocket. That was it all right, a copy of it anyway, minus the extra handwriting. He had practically memorized it months earlier.

Doug Stone and his family were not on either list, but the list had not gone away with the man he had stopped from shooting the mayor. The shooter was dead, the mayor lived, Jane was home safe, Doug was going to make it, some more bad guys were off the streets, but the list stared him in the face. Things weren't over yet.

With a world of questions whirling through his head, Sam drove back toward Kings County Hospital. It had been a long but productive night and he supposed that was why they were paid big bucks in the NYPD. He wanted to check in on Doug and share the joy of Jane's release, even if it was late. Doug, he was sure, would be too happy and relieved to sleep anyway.

The car's dash clock nudged 1:00 a.m. Visiting hours were long over, but he would extend the courtesy of asking the hospital anyway—the nurse's desk on Doug's floor specifically—if it would be all right to see Doug for a few minutes under a set of such unusual circumstances.

"I'm sorry, but Mr. Stone took his discharge into his own hands a while ago," the night duty nurse said. "He got out of bed, put on the pair of pants he came in here with, and wasn't taking no for an answer."

"That's Doug all right," Sam said.

"He said a car was making its way to the hospital for him at that very moment. His wife and daughter were in it, and they were all going home. Period. He would talk with his doctor in the morning," she said.

Sam put in a quick request to her for Doug's home address. She checked his chart, found it at the back, and slipped it to him, putting her index finger to her lips.

Sam had hardly pulled away from the hospital when he noticed a police car in the rear view. He automatically checked his speed—he wasn't speeding—and moved over to the right to let it pass, but instead the colored lights flashed on and began to strobe. Sam pulled to the side as the officer stepped out of his car. He watched the approach in the side view mirror.

Something felt wrong.

The glow from his break lights fell on the officer's boots. They were not the regulation issue worn by the department. His eyes traveled up the officer's legs to the gun in his holster. Also not the regulation snub nosed .38 Special.

Sam instinctively placed his hand on the .45 Luger that rested snugly near his chest holster, just in case. He was instructed by the officer to exit the vehicle, and as he did, he was certain things weren't right.

"What did I do wrong officer?"

"Shut up. Close the door and move over here. Put your hands on the hood of the car," the officer instructed.

"I have a right to know why you stopped me," Hurricane said walking slowly and memorizing the officer's features.

"Well, you see, Hurricane, I'm not here to just stop you; I'm here to put a real stop to you."

"Is that so? May I ask why?"

"You can ask, but I won't tell you. Now shut up and put your hands on the hood," he said giving Hurricane a shove.

"I was hoping you wouldn't say that, pal, but since you have, I'll tell you that you have made one very big mistake," Sam said.

"What's that? I have you dead to rights," he said.

"Maybe so, but you underestimated your opponent," Sam said.

"Don't try nothing funny because, by the time you move a muscle, I'll have shot you dead."

At the speed of light, Sam spun and hit his target with a roundhouse kick followed by a groin kick, and then an uppercut that sent him into dreamland. Sam used the fake officer's handcuffs and loaded him into Carol's car thinking that he might just get some much-needed information after all.

Sam's passenger was beginning to stir as he pulled up in front of the nearest precinct office. Two young officers were going into the building when Sam hailed them, "Hey, officers, could you help me get this guy inside please?"

As they came closer to the car, one of them said, "Hey, I can't believe it's you!"

"You who?" the other one asked as Sam hauled the handcuffed man out of the seat.

"It's Hurricane in the flesh."

"Yes, it's me, boys. Could you give me a hand?"

"What's this guy's story?" the other officer asked.

"He pulled me over and then threatened to kill me," Sam said.

"You're joking with us, right, Hurricane?" they said in unison.

"Nope. And now, Simmons and Anderson, from this point on, you call me Sam. All right?"

"Only if you call us Roy and Rich," Rich Anderson said.

They shook hands all around and then walked the impersonator inside.

"Why is it so quiet in here tonight?" Sam asked as he approached the booking desk.

"Well, Sam Rufus. I don't believe my eyes. How are you, you hound dog?" the man behind the counter said as he got up and limped around to shake hands.

"Charlie Wagner, I thought you would be retired by now," Sam said.

"I can't move around too much since I got my hips replaced, but I can do this desk job and the clerical stuff."

"It all needs doing," Sam said. "It's awfully good to see you again, Charlie. I know it's the middle of the morning, but isn't it unusually quiet in here?"

"Well, probably so. One of our own is being held hostage in his house. He came home from the hospital in one of our cars, and …"

"Wait a minute. Stop right there. You're not talking about Doug Stone, are you?" Sam asked.

"Sure am. It's the craziest story. Maloney was driving his beat when he got a call to pick up Doug's wife at Kings and then their daughter, and he was supposed to be taking them home."

"That's right, and Doug was set to be released from Kings in a few days," Sam said.

"Something like that, I guess. Maloney swung back by the hospital for Doug—that Doug can talk just about anybody into just about anything. Anyway, he wanted them all to go home together. Maloney was being a nice guy, walking everybody into the house. He was going to get them settled when he nearly got detained himself.

"They had a big surprise waiting for them inside, intruders with guns and everything. There were enough of them to be at least one-on-one, but they weren't interested in Maloney. They nabbed Doug and his wife and daughter and were holding them at gunpoint. Maloney couldn't draw his gun, not in that situation, so he just put his hands up and backed out the door the way he came in. He's in his car telling us all this on the radio when, all of a sudden, he goes missing. We haven't heard another peep from him, and we're out looking for him, too.

"Better tell us where this guy pulled you over. That could be Maloney's car, and our boy could be in the trunk or somewhere worse. Thanks to him, though, we've got Doug's place surrounded right now. How did you know it was Doug?"

"I was on my way over to his place before this joker pulled me over. Keep a close watch on him," Sam said.

"You know where you're going then?" Charlie said.

"I've got the address. Somewhere on Green Street, but don't bother with the details. It won't be hard to find with all the police cars around it," Sam said. "Charlie, I need a fast car with lights on it."

Charlie tossed him a set of keys. "Here, take number 22. It just came back from the shop. It's parked on the side."

Sam retrieved his duffle bag from Carol's car and went back into the police station.

"These are the keys to Doug Stone's car parked out front. Put it in a safe place for now, will you?" Sam asked, tossing them to Charlie.

"I'll do that Sam, and may God watch over you."

Sam headed out the door. He was driving as fast as he could with the siren blaring and the lights flashing. It wasn't long before Sam spotted Doug's house. He shut things down and pulled up to the first patrol car he saw blocking off the street.

"Hello, Sonny. What are we looking at here?" Sam asked.

"Hello, Sam. It doesn't look pretty from what I've picked up on the radio. It seems there are three people tied up inside. That would be Doug Stone, his wife, and his daughter. And there are four, maybe five, men from what we can tell. We think two are standing guard by the door, and we're not sure where the rest of them are, maybe holding a gun to Doug's head. That's all I know, Sam. I'm standing here waiting for orders like everyone else. If you want the whole story, you'll have to talk to Lieutenant Luther. He's the man in charge."

"Thank you, Sonny. You've been a big help. Back up a little, will you? I'll go in a little closer and check in with the lieutenant," Sam said.

Sam drove through a sea of police cars and turned his headlights off, too. He got out and walked over to the policemen congregating on the street near the front of the house. In the streetlights, he spotted John Luther.

"Hey, Lieutenant, what's the scoop?" he asked.

"Sam, what the hell are you doing here? Aren't you supposed to be on a thirty-day leave?"

"Yeah, well. After Doug got hit looking for his daughter, his wife found me at home about an hour after the judge was done with me. How, I really don't know, but she did. I called my shrink, and she gave me clearance to go on this mission. John, I hope I'm wrong, but I think this group of guys and the one I took out in Staten Island, not to mention the three I just left behind over at Ramshead could be working for the same person or people."

"What makes you think they're all affiliated?" the lieutenant asked.

"I found something really critical on one of the men I just left for dead that links them to the Staten Island killings. Somehow, all of this is related. Now, what's going on in there?" Sam asked.

"What do you know so far?"

"Just that Doug and his family are being held, and there are four or five men with guns," Sam said.

"We don't know any more than that. There have been no demands. We have not seen or heard from anyone directly, and we don't know if Doug and his family are dead or alive. We're just waiting, maybe until daylight, and deciding on a plan," Luther said.

"Let's take a look through these. These can detect images of heat-emanating objects through walls," Sam said, handing over a pair of advanced, forward-looking, infrared binoculars.

"It looks like Doug and his family are tied up and sitting together on the second floor. There are two men up and two men down. No, three men down. Here, take a look for yourself," the lieutenant said, handing the binoculars back to Sam.

"Lieutenant, have your men cause a little distraction out front, so I can make it around to the back of the house," Sam said.

"Sam, you're not even supposed to be here. If something goes wrong, it could cost me my stripes, not to mention my ass."

"Lieutenant, if we make it out of this alive, you can blame it all on me. But, either way, I'm going in, with or without your help. Doug asked me for my help, and I'm not going to turn my back on him now. I owe him that much."

"Okay, Sam, or should I call you 'Hurricane'? I think the world of Doug myself. He's helped me out of a few scrapes as well. He deserves a fighting chance. Except for me, you're the only one here with the experience to do this job. Give me a few minutes to set it up, and then head in and do what you do best," Lieutenant Luther said.

Sam waited for the lieutenant's thumbs up, and the distraction started. A couple of rookies staged a fight on the lawn, and the window blinds on either side of the front door parted. Sam made it to the side of the house where he found a tall rose trellis that reached almost up to a second-story window. That would be the room where Doug and his family were being held. He tested the trellis. It seemed sturdy enough. Rose thorns pierced his hands and wrists, but he climbed and persisted through the pain, praying all the while that the trellis would hold up under his weight.

When he reached the bottom of the window sill, he slowly inched himself up to a corner and peeked into the lighted room. Doug, Carol, and Jane were tied up and seated with their backs together in the middle of the floor. Doug faced the window straight on.

At least they are alive.

One man stood with his back to them looking out into the hallway. Sam took out his laser pen light, the one Doug had given him after they first became friends, and twirled the beam straight to Doug's eyes. Doug blinked and raised his eyes to the source. He knew without looking that Sam had come for him, and he had to think of some way to even out the odds.

"Hey, we're getting parched. Could we please get something to drink?" Doug asked the guard.

"I'll go get you some water, since it might be your last request," the man at the door said, laughing as he closed the door behind him.

Another guard stood to the side of an entertainment center. Sam had not seen him at first. He tapped on the window, and the guard came over and looked out but saw nothing. Then Sam tapped a little louder. This time, the guard opened the window to look out. Sam grabbed his gun and yanked him out of the window so fast he never had a chance to yell before hitting the ground. Luther's men could take him from there.

Sam entered the room, quickly untied everybody, and instructed them to stay where they were as he positioned himself behind the door. As the first man arrived with the water, he noticed his friend was gone and the window was open.

"Where's my buddy?" he asked.

"He found out he couldn't fly," was all Sam said as he delivered an open hand knife strike to the back of the man's head, knocking him out.

"Carol, can you and Jane climb down the rose trellis?" Sam asked. "Some officers outside will help you from there."

"I think we can make it," she said.

"Take a couple pair of socks and use them for gloves. Those vines are murder on your bare hands."

They did as instructed, Carol climbing out the window first while Doug hugged Jane and kept an eye on Carol descending the trellis. Jane went next, pale as a ghost and trembling. When Sam and Doug saw they had made it down safely, Doug traded his hospital gown for a shirt and said to Sam, "I think it's our turn to inflict some pain."

"Ten-four, partner," Sam said.

"Doug, take the guy's gun on the floor. He doesn't need it anymore. Tie him up and put something in his mouth to keep him quiet. Check the rest of the upstairs. I'll venture down. If you see anyone, and they threaten your life, shoot to kill. We ought to try, though, to keep someone alive so we can get some answers. The plot's been thickening since we last talked."

Slowly, Sam opened the bedroom door and made his way out into the hallway. When he made it down to the first floor, he spotted two figures in what would be the front living room. He thought he heard someone talking or humming in the kitchen. The door was slightly ajar, and he saw the back of a person standing at the counter preparing food. Sam nudged the door a bit, just in case someone was standing behind it. Then he slowly made his way into the kitchen staying low to the floor.

"Roger, are you trying to sneak up on me?" a female voice spoke.

"More like a Hurricane," Sam said.

As she turned around, Sam popped up, grabbed her arm, and held his gun close to her face but pointing at the ceiling. "Settle down, sister, and be quiet, or I'll drop you right here," he said. "How many more of you are in this house?" Sam asked.

"Four. Two out there and two upstairs," she said.

"How many more are in the basement?" Sam tested her.

"I didn't know there was a basement, and, as far as I know, there's just the five of us total. They brought me along to fix them something to eat while they hung out for a while."

"Do they all have weapons?"

"Yes, I think so from what I saw. I was riding in the back of the van, so I'm not for sure. I don't know much about guns, and I don't particularly want to learn. What I know is there are four hungry people waiting for breakfast."

"What are they doing here?"

"Waiting for someone. Chris Cobalt. He's supposed to be here around seven o'clock."

"Why would a drug dealer want to come to a cop's house?" Sam asked.

"What do you mean 'drug dealer', 'cop's house'? These are drug enforcement men. My friend Roger is one of them, and they're setting up a sting. They parked the van a half block down and had me wait there until they were sure the coast was clear in here. Once Chris gets here, the drops, the hand-offs, and everything else is supposed to be going on over the next several hours. Our guys are going to be here, laying low and taking the druggies down and out quietly one at a time. But now I don't know what's going to happen. Roger said the place is crawling out front with cops, and nobody in their right mind is going to come close now."

Sam took his badge out and showed it to her.

"I hate to inform you, but Roger and the rest of your pals are on the opposite end of drug enforcement, and they're here attempting to harm the policeman and his family who live here and to extort money from them. Do you understand that?"

"What? No way. You've got it wrong. I've been with Roger for five years. I thought this …"

"Never mind what you thought."

"But if this is a cop's house and Roger's doing what you say he's doing, I'm helping commit a crime."

"That's right, you are. Hang on a minute. What's your name?"

"I'm Linda. But if Roger and these guys aren't DEA, what did you say they're doing now?"

"The cop who lives here busted a for-real drug boss years ago. The man had killed two people who were running from him, and he's due to die in about 24 hours. The guy you're expecting at seven o'clock and a few other guys, like your friend Roger, are in with a few higher-ups doing bigger things. They kidnapped the cop's daughter, the one being held upstairs, and were holding her for ransom. That was until they met me, and their plans took a quick detour. The daughter got out of their grasp just in time to return home to this mess."

"This is a cop's family? Are you sure he's not a drug dealer?" Linda asked again.

"Yes, and if you cooperate with me, I'll tell the police you helped me. How would you like to right a wrong, Linda?" Sam asked.

"I would, as long as I don't get arrested," she said.

"Fair enough. Are you sure I can trust you?"

"Yes."

"Okay, let's think. How are you going to take the food in to them?"

"I was going to load everything onto this food cart and push it down to the den."

"How much longer before the food is good to go?"

"Just a few minutes," she said.

"See if you can find a tablecloth to make a hanging skirt around the bottom of the cart. I'll sneak in on the other side of it as you wheel it in. Try to act like nothing's up, or they might hurt you," Sam said.

Linda found table linens in the pantry. She threw a tablecloth over the cart, piled on a platter of bacon and sausages, muffins, and a pot of coffee. Then she started down the hall. When she was just about inside the den, she called up the stairs and into the den, "Breakfast is ready."

"It's about time. I'm so darn hungry I could eat a bear," one man said coming away from the front window.

Both men put their guns down and went to the cart just as Sam burst into view holding his gun on them.

"Who the hell are you?" they asked.

"I'm the one who's going to send you to jail where you belong, but first, I need a few answers," Sam said.

"Do you really think you can take all of us, copper? If so, I think you've been watching too many John Wayne movies, and the only way I'll tell you anything is over my dead body."

"If that is your wish, then so be it." Sam pulled the trigger and shot him where he stood. "How about you, jack? How talkative are you feeling?" Sam asked.

Roger looked toward the stairs for relief but saw only Linda and Doug Stone standing there.

"You can't kill us in cold blood. You're a cop!"

"You seem pretty sure of yourself," Sam said as he put his gun back into his holster. "Tell you what, Roger—it is Roger, isn't it?—you go for your gun, and I'll go for mine, and we'll see who's a faster draw. If you win, you walk away, but if not, you'll leave your insides scattered all over this room. The choice, as they say, is yours."

"You'll shoot me before I touch my gun."

"I would rather talk to you than shoot you."

"I've got nothing to say to you."

"Roger, please don't do anything foolish," Linda pleaded. "You can get yourself out of this and cooperate with the police. I know everything. Please, Roger."

"Baby, not you. Not now," Roger said.

"You better listen to her because, if you draw, you will never know how things turn out, because you'll be the one I kill no matter what happens next. I'll probably see you in hell, and we'll continue our little game there," Sam said.

Just then, Sam saw in the mirror a man creeping down the stairs in back of Doug. Sam turned and fired once, hitting him in the head dead center. Roger tried to pick up his gun, and Sam sent two bullets in his direction. One hit him in the neck and sent him flying back into the wall.

"Freeze, Hurricane, or I'll drop your friend!" Linda cried as she pulled a pistol and leveled it on Doug.

"What's this, Linda? I thought I could trust you."

Before she could answer, the front door was kicked in, and police stormed the house. They took Linda's gun and cuffed her and started to handcuff Sam before Doug ordered them to stop.

"But he shot these people!" a young officer said.

"I know what he did, Officer Drummond. He's working under cover on a special mission," Doug replied. "This is just between us. Do I make myself clear?"

"Yes, sir! Clear as glass, sir," Officer Drummond said. He took off the handcuffs and apologized to Sam.

"No need to apologize. You were only doing your job," Sam said.

Daylight had arrived, and Sam checked his watch.

"Linda here told me that Chris Cobalt was expected to be here at seven o'clock," Sam told Doug and Lieutenant Luther. "That's about now, and I happen to know that Chris will not be making it this morning or any other morning. I left him in a rather ugly heap not too long after Jane went home. He must have had these guys set up to come over as a little extra insurance to be sure things went smooth by the time he arrived. I assume he was coming to pick up the cash."

"That is what this is all about. Isn't that what you think, Doug? Chris Cobalt and a few of his friends kidnapped your daughter for a dual prize—money and Wallace's freedom. They planned to collect a $250,000 ransom before Grady Wallace was to be injected, and probably hold on to Jane after the money was collected until somehow Wallace got sprung, or off, or something. Except, their hostage got away, they didn't pick up the money, and Wallace is still going down. If we're right, and Jane happens to be the person close to you they wanted to die if Grady dies, doesn't it make sense that somebody's got something else up their sleeve about keeping Grady alive? Maybe this is the end of the line though. Seven men have died in less than ten hours. Who's left standing to see it through?"

"And who else is on the right side of the law that they could possibly want at such a late hour?" Doug asked. Hey! What about the judge who sent Grady Wallace to meet his maker?"

Memory of the list hit Sam like a lightning bolt. "Grogan. Was it Judge Charles Grogan that sentenced him, Doug?" Sam asked.

"Yes, that's him. I'm sure it is. How did you know?"

"He seems to be a pretty unpopular guy with the Wallace family. I'll tell you about that later. He's also the same one who told me I was too violent. I wonder what he would be thinking right about now. I know what I'm thinking. Grogan could be more than one man's target, and I think we need to get over there and give him some protection before somebody else goes after him."

"You could be right, Sam. I just hope we make it before anything bad happens."

Chapter Sixteen

Doug left the disaster that had been his home in search of Carol and Jane. He found them in the back seat of a squad car with a young officer standing by. He asked the officer to have someone stay near them for the next 24 hours and to alert his precinct of his location.

"Are you all right?" Doug asked, opening the back door and squatting down to their eye level.

"We're fine, or we're going to be," Carol said. "But you, you're still so weak. You don't need to be out here doing this."

Jane rested against her mother and twisted a rope of her hair between her thumb and index finger. Her eyes questioned Doug, doubted him, and perhaps blamed him. He saw how seriously she was rattled, and it broke his heart.

"I'm fine, and we're all going to be fine once this is all over, I promise. But right now, I need to go with Sam for a little while. Listen to me. I need you both to go over to Mary's house. I'm sure she's up after all this commotion. This officer or another one is going to be close by you until I get back. Ask Mary if she'll fix you some breakfast and put you up in the guestroom for a few hours. Then call my sis and make arrangements for all of us to stay a little while at the lake house if it's vacant. I don't want either of you going back in there," he motioned with his head, "under any circumstance. Do you understand?"

"Yes. Understand," Carol said.

"Jane? You know I love you both very much, and I'll see you in a few hours. This will be over soon, and we're all going to be all right."

Sam took in the scene of Doug with his family. Love and a bond like that was something he wanted for himself some day, minus this particular trauma. He walked over to the car and nodded to Carol and Jane. Words wouldn't come, and there wasn't time for them anyway. He turned and walked quickly to his car. Doug was right behind him.

"And where do you think you are going?"

"With you, Sam. If any of these bastards are still standing, I owe them a payback. With you back as my partner, this might be my only chance," Doug said.

"All right, Doug, but we don't know what we're getting into. It may be nothing but a wild goose chase, but my stomach's talking to me again. In the event something's going down at the judge's house and the shooting starts, you need to stay out of it. You're not exactly in crime-fighting condition, and I don't want to have to worry about you," Sam said.

They got in car 22, and Sam handed Doug the note.

"Here's why I'm sure Grogan's a marked man. He put both Sidney and Grady Wallace behind bars. A few hours ago, I learned there was a connection between Grady Wallace and Chris Cobalt. I heard that Chris Cobalt was behind kidnapping Jane. Both Chris Cobalt and his brother Jim pushed with Grady for a while. Both of them were approved by the Bureau of Prisons to visit Sidney Wallace, Grady's brother, and they visited him pretty regularly. This note was on Chris Cobalt's body that's on its way to the morgue right now. It's the same hit list that was on the man I shot in Staten Island six months ago. The guy was taking down the jury and working his way up the list to the judge. But I thought things were over when he was. Grogan's address is on there, isn't it? He's in Manhattan, isn't he?" Sam asked.

"Yes, I'm pretty sure I know where this is."

Sam switched the lights and siren on, and they raced through the light Saturday morning traffic. At the rate they were traveling, it wouldn't take long to reach the judge's house. It was now pushing eight o'clock, and Sam hadn't slept in 36 hours. He was all jangled nerves and adrenalin, on a mission, in his mind if nowhere else, to save Judge Grogan.

"What time is Grady Wallace's execution?" Sam asked.

"Soon," Doug said.

Doug called the dispatcher on the radio and told her to have Sergeant Rogers of Manhattan's 125th precinct call him on his cell phone. "Tell him it's an emergency."

"I hope you're right about this, Sam, or I could be joining you in the unemployment line," Doug said.

"That was good thinking, calling ahead, Doug, and don't worry about losing your job. There's always room for top-notch security guards," Sam chuckled.

Doug's phone rang.

"Doug Stone? This is Sergeant Rogers, how can I be of service?"

"Sergeant, can you confirm Judge Charles Grogan's home address for me? I show 108 West High Avenue."

"Sure, give me a minute. The dispatcher said this is some kind of an emergency. What's going on?"

"We believe the judge is in imminent danger. We're heading for the address now and need to confirm that it's accurate. I'm calling you because I'm pretty sure this is in your precinct," Doug said.

"If it's here in our precinct, we should be handling this. Why are you so interested?" Rogers asked.

Sam took the phone from Doug.

"Rick, this is Hurricane. We have reason to believe there may be some bad guys at work this morning at the judge's house. They're linked with the guy I killed in Staten Island, and there seems to be a significant number of them out there. Doug and I are in a patrol car now with the lights and sirens going, but we'll have to cruise in quietly when we near Judge Grogan's. We're concerned whoever this is may have killing the judge in mind, and we don't want to be the ones to set them off," Sam said.

"They wouldn't kill a judge, would they?" Rogers asked.

"The same group killed eight people in Staten Island and kidnapped Doug Stone's daughter. I'm not willing to take that chance, are you?" Sam asked.

"Negative, and we've just confirmed the High Avenue address. We're practically around the corner," Rogers said.

"Can you send an unmarked car over there right away and let us know if there's anything that doesn't look or feel right? We should be there shortly, probably another ten to fifteen minutes. Don't wait for us," Hurricane said.

"All right, but what if they make a move before you get there?" Rogers asked Sam.

"Then do what we do best, and take him down at any cost, if you have to!" Sam yelled.

Charles Grogan had seen his wife off at LaGuardia the previous evening for a trip to New Orleans where she would speak on behalf of the American Red Cross. He was proud of her volunteer efforts and how she had been involved in their sons' schools and other local and national efforts. She was a born leader, and she would be in her element.The boys and he could fend for themselves just fine for a few days.

That same night, very late, Jimmy Cobalt had tried to reach his brother by phone. He didn't answer, and neither did Toby Sanders or Steve Swenson. He knew of the tentative plans to take down the Stone girl, and he knew the ransom money had come together, and he was fairly certain they were going to be able to get their hands on it the next morning.

He had driven to Ramshead, and when he saw the area before the construction site blocked off by police and emergency vehicles, he turned around and went to the home he had shared with his brother. He would watch the news, and he would watch his back. He would also move forward with the final plan, brother or no brother. He called Roger and told him Chris might not be there, but he was to gather the reinforcements, go in, and find the money. When he next checked, Roger and his team of four were getting ready to move in on the Stone's house.

In the middle of the morning when all self-respecting citizens were deep in sleep, Jimmy Cobalt and another group of four men disabled the home security system at 108 West High Avenue. They slipped inside the impressive two-story stone structure undetected and unannounced. It was easier than they had anticipated, and now it was time for the grand plan to unfold.

"When we're done with this one and meet up with Roger for the cash, we will have earned some time off," Jimmy told them. "Let's go."

Three of them drew their guns. The fourth did not. They took the wide polished marble stairs in perfect silence. Jimmy waited on ground level.

The Grogans had been surprised, of course, shaken from the depths of their dreams by the pressure of heavy metal roughly twisting on their temples, and then the horror of realizing someone was there in their bedroom with a gun to their head, and then the sound of the instrument being cocked, ready to fire. They would comply.

"Get up. Hold still."

A second person appeared from behind the first, quickly binding them with tape and cord. A strip of duct tape guaranteed silence. It also guaranteed removing half the skin from one's face if carelessly removed, but that would be a bridge to cross later. The smooth cord bound their hands behind their backs. The teenaged boys were prodded down the stairs in their underwear by their own would-be executioner and were joined by their father.

Jimmy had rearranged the formal dining room. Three high-backed chairs had been pulled from the table. The boys' hands remained tied behind their backs and they were each seated and bound to a chair around the chest. The judge sat alone facing them wearing his blue pajamas with the monogrammed pocket, his legs tied separately to the chair legs. Beside the judge's chair stood a small end table with a telephone.

The boys' eyes were filled with terror as they looked from their father to each of the five men. A man blindfolded the boys and removed a cloth gag from the judge's mouth. The five men stood in a semi-circle looking at the scene before them and said nothing.

"What is it you want? Why are you doing this?" Judge Grogan asked.

"I'm Jimmy Cobalt," he said and stepped in front of the judge. "Does that name ring a bell? How about my brother, Chris Cobalt? How about Sid and Grady Wallace? Do any of us mean anything to you?"

Judge Grogan vaguely remembered the names, but had to think for a while about the cases. He had so many over the years that they all ran together at times. "Oh, yes, I recall a Jim Cobalt. You and your brother were running with that Wallace guy, Grady Wallace, and his operation," the judge replied.

"That's right, Your Honor, and you're the righteous son of a bitch that wanted to make sure none of us ever breathed free air again. No wonder you're number one on the shit list. Number one, you smug bastard. How does that feel! In case you don't remember, Grady's supposed to die at eleven o'clock this morning. We would hate to see that happen because, if it does, your boys here are going to join him in paradise. And after you get a good up-close look at your bloody boys winging their way to heaven, I'll put you out of your misery," Jimmy said.

"Grady Wallace killed two people in cold blood, and there's no telling how many zombies are out there because of the mind-wasting poison he peddles. His brother's a loser, too. Any man who beats his wife and child within an inch of their life is no good trash. Both of these men deserve the sentence they got. You know that. I know you know that. You're not a stupid man. Yet, you choose to hang with bad people, Jimmy. Think about it. You and your brother, there's no telling how many people you have both killed in smaller, slower ways. Drugs waste them a breath at a time. Evidence tampering, you both got off on evidence tampering. What a sham.

Jimmy Cobalt's fist stopped the judge, and the boys bucked back in their seats at the sound.

"We weren't talking about my brother and me. We were talking about Grady Wallace. We're talking about you picking up this phone and calling whoever you need to call to stay his execution," Jimmy said. He took a knife from his pocket and cut the cord on the judge's wrists. "That would be your pal, the governor. Now dial."

"I can't do that," the judge said.

120

"Now, Judge Grogan, I think you know the governor of the state of New York. I think you know each other on a real personal basis. I think you're friends, buddies even. I think you've got his home phone number, and he wouldn't mind getting a call from you so early in the morning. He might think you're calling to play a little golf like you did last Saturday. Or maybe you've called him before for a little favor here and a little favor there. Isn't that how it works with you big shots? Playing a little card game with peoples' lives? Well, it's long past time to deal me into the game."

"You'll never get away with this, Jimmy," the judge said.

"I'm not asking to get away with anything. It's not me I'm worried about right now. The clock's ticking, and you, Judge, are wasting valuable time. You need to be buying time instead. I'm going to ask you one more time to pick up the phone and call the gov and buy a little time for our friend Grady, or I'm going to have to hurt one of your boys."

The other men looked on. Judge Grogan looked from Jimmy to his men for confirmation or denial of what Jimmy had just said.

Jimmy instructed three men to keep an eye on the front, rear, and basement entrances of the house. One man would stay with him.

"Look, Jimmy, why don't you just forget about this whole thing? You're free as a bird. You and your men can just turn around and leave. We won't tell anybody what happened here," Judge Grogan said.

"That's real nice of you, but no thanks. Now pick up the phone."

The judge made no move. Jimmy reached into his pants pocket, snapped open a switchblade, and slashed the naked chest of the judge's youngest son. The boy, squealing under the tape as blood streamed from him, thrashed to be free of his chair.

The judge went white with rage and horror.

"Jeremy!" he called.

He could barely manage to look, but he had to. His son was suffering and possibly dying in front of him, and he could not turn away from him, not now. He was powerless to save him, powerless to help him, even powerless to comfort him. His son, his precious son. And what must his other son be enduring at this moment? He couldn't reach him either.

"You see, Judge Grogan, I don't kid around," Jimmy said. "Now get on the phone before I take care of the other one."

"I don't have his number memorized. It's programmed into my cell phone, and that's on my dresser."

"Go get the phone, Jason. Double doors at the end of the hall upstairs."

When Sam and Doug arrived at the address, they saw an unmarked car with two men parked two doors before the house and another car with two men a few doors beyond it. They flashed their headlights to indicate they were there. Sam drove the car slowly past the judge's house while Doug looked through the FUR binoculars.

"It looks like several people in a cluster on the lower level, one upstairs, and two others down near what would be front and rear entrances. That's all I can tell," Doug said.

Doug's phone rang, "Hello, Doug Stone."

"Doug, this is Sergeant Rogers. I'm in the car you just passed. Things look quiet from the outside, but we believe there is a concentration of bodies on the ground level, maybe six or seven people. It's possible the judge and his family have company for the weekend, and they're all up and having breakfast together, or getting ready to."

"We're still convinced Judge Grogan is in real trouble. Let's see what we need to do to make sure the judge is safe or to make sure he gets out of this alive in the event something's going down," Doug said.

"What's the game plan?" Sergeant Rogers asked.

"Are you sure you counted six people? I couldn't get a count myself. There's a mass of bodies in a downstairs room, and I didn't want to get out of the squad car and knock on the door, although, that may not be a bad idea," Doug said.

"Sam, did you hear that?"

Doug turned to Sam, but he had stopped the car and was walking swiftly down the Street with his duffle bag slung over his shoulder.

"Sergeant Rogers, Hurricane is going in. You might want to call in a few more men and get ready to charge the house when he gives the signal," Doug said.

"What's the signal?" Sergeant Rogers asked.

"I'm not sure myself, but I have a feeling as soon as he starts something, we will know. Cover the front, and send two men around back for now. If anyone comes out, don't let them get away. And one more thing. If they give us no choice, we shoot to kill," Doug said.

Hurricane's watch read nearly nine o'clock. In a few hours, Grady Wallace was scheduled to get a much-deserved lethal injection. He took a mental inventory, trying to keep a clear head in his sleep-deprived condition. Doug Stone was alive and with him, but he must be careful to keep Doug out of the most direct danger. Carol and Jane were with their neighbor and being protected by an officer. And now the judge and his family should be the last of it, he hoped.

What Sam did not know was that the judge had called the governor and pleaded with him to issue a stay of execution for Grady Wallace. The governor had been reluctant. He hated buckling to a hostile situation, but he was certain that Judge Grogan and his remaining son needed to live, and he was just as certain that justice would be exacted from Grady Wallace— if not now, then later. He would issue the order and put the wheels in motion, but it might already be too late. People and procedures were in place. He would call the judge back as soon as he received confirmation that Grady Wallace was returned to his cell unharmed and would stay that way. When the governor ended the call with Judge Grogan, he got on the phone with NYPD and alerted them to the situation at Judge Grogan's. Within minutes the neighborhood would be covered in blue.

Sam cut the small distance between houses to the rear of the two story house. Unlike Doug's house, there was no way to access the upper level, and the ground-floor windows were at least two feet over his head. He spotted a stone walkway that was partially concealed and angled into the ground and led to a lower elevation of the house. The walkway terminated at a door with stained glass panes. He pulled his jacket sleeve over his hand and released a blunt chop to one of the glass panes. He reached through, turned the knob, and entered the basement.

Nothing was happening down below. He returned to the outside door and waited for Doug to discover him. From his duffle, he equipped himself with what he thought he could use, and then handed the .357 Magnum to Doug when he appeared.

"Against my better judgment, but here," Sam said.

Simultaneously, Sam and Doug saw a pair of legs coming down the stairs. A pistol was visible at waist level. Sam and Doug stepped into a shadow and froze. The man spotted the broken glass. Not wanting to fire his weapon and call attention to themselves, Sam hurled two eight-point ninja stars that caught the man in his neck and temple. He dropped to the floor with a thud.

"That was a lucky break," Doug said. "I know you hated doing that, but I didn't see another way either. Let's get upstairs."

Sam went first, expecting to come out into a kitchen or utility room. Instead, it opened into an immense and elegantly appointed living room. Its walls were covered with paintings in ornate frames, one wall was a library with floor-to-ceiling shelves. There were chairs and lamps for reading, seating areas for conversation, a grand piano, vases of flowers and objects of art everywhere. His eyes moved around the room and stopped on a man who was looking out into the courtyard.

Hurricane and Doug moved into the room toward him as he saw their reflections in the glass. He whirled around to face them, but Hurricane was on him with a wrist-lock that caused him to drop his gun, and Doug held the Magnum to his head.

"One peep out of you, and you're a dead man. Do you understand?"

The man, Chuck, nodded.

"Show me on your fingers how many more of you bad guys are here," Hurricane said.

Chuck held up four fingers as Doug bent over to pick up his gun.

"Make that three. Doug, take this guy downstairs by his friend, and make sure he stays quiet and out of the way."

Doug moved Chuck down the stairs. His wrists were cuffed behind him, and the .357 Magnum was planted firmly in the back of his neck. The sight of ninja stars sticking out of his friend's head made Chuck sick to his stomach. He started to retch when Doug turned him away from the body and gagged him for real. He sat him on the floor with his legs straddling a support post and tied them at the ankles.

Quiet and out of the way—check.

Doug was about to rejoin Hurricane upstairs when he came down with another man at gunpoint. "Here's one more. The judge and two more of these guys are in the dining room," he said.

The man acknowledged Chuck on the floor, then looked at Doug as Sam moved him to another support post.

"What are you guys, a couple of knights in shining armor come over here to help the judge? Are you crazy? Do you realize who we are?"

"No, I don't know who you are. Please educate me," Hurricane said pressing him into a kneeling position.

"I'm Hank the Hammer. They call me that 'cause of my hands. Bam! My hands work like lightning. I don't need no weapon. No, sir, I'm against 'em. My hands can kill a man, please a woman, and make a ham and cheese sandwich all at the same time and quicker than you can say jack rabbit.

"Now the boss man, I don't really know him personally, but I know he's got some power. He's more powerful than the President of the United States, and he's got more money than all the people combined and living right here in the Big Apple. He's going to make me a rich man. He knows how to lead men, and he's got plans to right this world the way it is suppose to be."

"How is the world supposed to be, Hank?" Hurricane asked, taking out a pair of handcuffs.

"It's supposed to be perfect. Perfect in his image, that's what. And we're helping make it that way. We're going to wipe out all the useless people, the ones who can't work or won't work—the handicapped, the retired, the people livin' off unemployment and suckin' up disability—and we're going to wipe out those who don't do right unto others."

"Now, wait a minute, pal," Hurricane said. "Most people would be working if they could. A lot of those people you talked about have made a good contribution to this country. It isn't entirely their fault that jobs started leaving our shores. I'm afraid this is just the beginning. Things are going to get tougher for everybody, yourself included, before they get better. So, what about it? What about you, Hammer? Instead of killing people, shouldn't you be trying to do something a little more positive to help better the situation?"

"We are. We're helping those people by putting them out of their misery and frustration. And that judge up there, Judge Jackass, or whatever his name is, he's a menace to society. There's nothin' else to be said 'bout him. He's putting the wrong guys away and setting them up to die, and he's keeping the real dangerous people out running around on the streets collecting welfare. He's a careless man, and we're here to teach him a lesson. Now, if you don't let me get back to work and untie Chuck my buddy here, I'm going to have to put my hands on you and turn you and your friend into a couple statistics."

"But, Hank, you haven't told me who your leader is yet. He sounds intriguing to me, like somebody I would like to meet. If you're going to turn me into a statistic, what harm would it do to tell me your leader's name?" Hurricane said.

"Why do you want to know so bad? No, sir, no. I changed my mind. You're toying with me, and now I'm going to put you in your grave wondering what his name is," he said grabbing for Hurricane's feet.

Hurricane came down with a hammer fist on Hank's neck. There was an avalanche of cracking bones as Hank slumped over.

"We don't have time for his shenanigans. Keep an eye on him and make sure he's secured, in the event he wakes up. I'm going upstairs."

Hurricane walked up the basement stairs and toward the dining room.

"Jason, go and scrape up some food for me while we're waiting for the governor to call his friend back," Jimmy said.

"What sounds good?" Jason asked.

"Anything. What's in the kitchen, Judge? Or isn't that your domain? Bring me a Diet Coke, and I'll think about it," Jimmy said.

Hurricane had made his way to the kitchen and was waiting for his guest to appear.

Jason was whistling until the kitchen door swung closed and he saw Hurricane sitting on the counter with his gun pointed at him.

"Surprised?" Sam asked.

"How did you get in here?" Jason asked.

"How many more of you are in the house?" Sam asked.

"That's for me to know and you to find out, but you're not too smart, are you? If you shoot me now, Jimmy will automatically blow the judge's head off," Jason smirked.

"Good point," Sam responded. "Maybe I'll just use this instead." He came off the stool and thrust his knife into Jason's rib cage. Jason bent forward and tried to remove the knife as Sam held it firmly in place and lowered him to the floor.

A phone rang in the dining room.

"Answer it," Jimmy said picking it up and handing it to Judge Grogan.

Sam picked up a tray, threw on some items from the refrigerator, and headed to the dining room with the tray in front of his face as Judge Grogan finished the call.

"It's done," the judge said looking at Jimmy. "Grady Wallace just had his life spared. But you're not getting away with this, Jimmy Cobalt."

Hurricane moved the tray away from his face for an instant and made his way a little farther into the room. Judge Grogan thought he was seeing a mirage.

"Shut up, Judge," Jimmy said. "You may have just done one thing right, but there's a whole list of shit you can't ever make right. You can't bring my brother back, and I'm thinking maybe I'll send you over to the other side to have a little talk with him in person. How would you like that?" He brought the gun barrel to the judge's forehead and clicked a cartridge into place.

The judge's son jerked his body forward in his chair toward the sound and fell face forward into the back of Jimmy's legs at the same moment that Sam came up beside them.

"Hey!" Sam yelled from a couple of feet away.

Jimmy turned.

Sam lunged forward using the tray as a shield to move Jimmy's hand away from the judge's face.

Jimmy didn't realize it wasn't Jason until it was too late. He swung his gun just as Sam grabbed him and threw him across the floor.

"Let's see how tough you really are without your friends here to help," Sam said.

Jimmy tried to blindside Hurricane, but he found out how quickly this Hurricane could move. Hurricane ducked Jimmy's fist and hit him with a powerful elbow strike in his belly. When Jimmy bent over, Hurricane came up with an uppercut that sent him flying through the front window and into the yard.

"This must be the sign," Sergeant Rogers said to the growing number of NYPD. "Let's move in."

Hurricane walked out through the broken window, not letting Jimmy out of his sight.

Jimmy stood up, bleeding from his mouth. "You're a strong one, aren't you? Let's see what else you've got!"

Jimmy tried to release a roundhouse kick, but Hurricane squatted low and swept Jimmy's planted foot out from underneath him, sending the back of his head down hard on the ground. When Jimmy staggered up, Hurricane gave him four combination kicks, two to the ribs and two to the side of his head. He kicked so fast the police saw only the last kick before the body hit the ground.

Hurricane squatted next to Jimmy arid said, "Look, too many people have been getting hurt needlessly around here lately. Why don't you tell me what's going on so you don't end up like your brother. What are you trying to prove?

"Screw you," Jimmy said sitting up and drawing back his fist. Hurricane caught it and gave it a twist behind Jimmy's back that sent him crawling into the trunk of a large maple.

"Jimmy, I'm beginning to run out of patience. I want to know who your boss is. More specifically, I want to know what you're up to with Sid and Grady Wallace."

When there was no response, Hurricane planted a fist in his stomach. Blood spurted from Jimmy's mouth.

"Try again," Hurricane said, "I didn't hear you."

Jimmy wheezed and tried to catch his breath, "Brothers helping brothers. That's all you need to know."

Hurricane wanted more, and he was going to keep getting it, until the judge came through the front door with the paramedics.

"All right, Sam, I think he's had enough."

Hurricane stood back as Jimmy wobbled to his feet. Judge Grogan stepped closer and approached Jimmy who looked like he was done for, but then clumsily hurled himself into the judge sending them both staggering. Jimmy got one arm around the judge's neck and pulled a gun from his boot with the other.

"Everybody back up, or I kill the judge," Jimmy said.

Time froze.

Jimmy rasped his bloody breath into the judge's ear, "You see, judge? You and your cronies underestimate us."

"Your Honor, what do you want me to do?" Hurricane asked.

"Can you take him, Sam?"

Jimmy's arm clenched the judge's neck tighter. "Even if you kill me here, there will be more of us coming, sooner or later. You have no idea of our numbers. We're not stopping until freedom rings and the debt's been paid."

"'Hurricane', Judge. Today, it's 'Hurricane', and hell, yes, I can take him," Hurricane said.

"Then take the bastard down."

Before Jimmy knew what hit him, he lost his grip on the judge and went sailing backward. His arm had been nearly ripped free of his body. Hurricane had drawn and fired his .44 so quickly that no one knew what happened until Jimmy was set back on his heels and crashed to the ground. He grunted and tried to get up, but before he could, Hurricane grabbed him and threw him to the side. Again, he tried to stand and then spotted his gun. He made his move to get it. When Jimmy picked up his gun with a clumsy left hand and attempted to fire, Sam was ready and emptied his pistol into Jimmy's body.

The police moved in, and Judge Grogan looked at Sam and said, "Thank you for saving my life. I owe you an apology."

"All in the line of duty, Your Honor," Sam said.

"Your suspension has been dropped, and you are free to go back to work when you're ready," Judge Grogan said.

Doug had administered first aid and stayed with the boys until the paramedics arrived. Now he walked over to Sam and the judge.

"Thanks just the same, Judge, but I think from here on, I'm going to freelance as a private investigator. Maybe I'll even consider having a partner, someone I know very well. What would you say to that, Doug?"

Doug smiled and shook Sam's hand. "That sounds very good to me, partner."

Two rookies who had watched the scene from the sidewalk came over to the judge and asked, "Who is that guy, anyway?"

"Why that, my young crime fighters, is the Hurricane."

Meet the Author

Joseph J. Cacciotti

Joseph Cacciotti grew up in Racine, Wisconsin, along the shores of Lake Michigan. His desire to write appeared early in life when his high school teachers encouraged him to write poetry and to become a journalist. His drive to write fiction grew stronger as he matured.

Joe made a promise to his friend and mentor, Harold A. Schink, on his deathbed. Harold asked Joe to never stop writing. Joe has been faithful to that promise. In 2006, he published *Poems for the Heart*, an award-winning collection of fifty of his most talked about poems. His second poetry book, *Poems for the Heart, Volume II* was released in April 2012.

Also published in 2006 was *Blue Collar Real Estate Mogul*, a biography based on true life experiences that he and his best friend endured as landlords in Racine and about a friendship that never stopped growing, even after death.

Joe began writing his "Hurricane" books in 2009, a series about "Hurricane" Samuel James Rufus, an unconventional detective whose methods for getting the bad guys come close to crossing ethical and legal lines in his pursuit of justice. *Hurricane Cores the Big Apple,* the first in the series is now in its second release. The second book in the Hurricane series, *Hurricane Rocks Wisconsin*, was released in March 2012. *Hurricane Strips Las Vegas* is the third book in the series. Several more adventures are underway and will be released soon.

Joe lives with his wife Diane in Racine, Wisconsin. They have three daughters. Joe continues to write poetry, as well as the "Hurricane Sam Rufus" adventures.

www.ingramcontent.com/pod-product-compliance
Lightning Source LLC
Chambersburg PA
CBHW060428260626
47161CB00005B/1826